SHOOTING SCRIPT AND OTHER MYSTERIES

By William Link and Richard Levinson

Richard Levinson and William Link (seated), circa 1962.

SHOOTING SCRIPT AND OTHER MYSTERIES

By William Link and Richard Levinson

Introduction by Joseph Goodrich
Foreword by Tom Straw

CRIPPEN & LANDRU PUBLISHERS
Cincinnati, Ohio
2021

For information contact:

Crippen & Landru, Publishers

P. O. Box 532057

Cincinnati, OH 45253 USA

Web: www.crippenlandru.com

E-mail: Info@crippenlandru.com

ISBN (softcover): 978-1-936363-58-2

ISBN (clothbound): 978-1-936363-59-9

First Edition: October 2021

10 9 8 7 6 5 4 3 2 1

CONTENTS

MAKING MAGIC OUT OF MURDER

It makes perfect sense that Richard Levinson and William Link were magicians. And not figuratively. They were actual magicians, something they had in common when they met in junior high school in Elkins Park outside Philadelphia. According to Link, on the first day there his friends told him to "look out for a tall guy who loved murder mysteries and did magic." Meanwhile, Levinson was alerted to "look out for a short guy who loved murder mysteries and did magic." Fated by geography and those shared passions, the two became friends that day, and would go on to make magic out of murder for decades to come.

In those teenage years they would meet every day after school and write stories. Radio dramas were big then, and they tuned in to *Suspense* and *Escape*. Then they would write radio plays and gather friends in their garages on Saturdays to act them out.

They also started writing short stories. Anyone familiar with the top echelon writing in their television scripts will see that same maturity of craft in their young efforts appearing here in this collection. From the start Levinson and Link wrote *up*. They engaged their audience on a high level of challenge, as if to say, "We're not going to talk down to you. What we're going to do is engage you."

A taste for engagement derived from their own voracious appetites for crime literature. Moving on from the Hardy Boys, they read authors that Link called their university of mystery writing: Ellery Queen, John Dickson Carr, and G. K. Chesterton. Young Dick and Bill studied detective stories of the 1930s and 1940s to learn structure and how to advance plot through character. Then they read further back – to 1912 – and discovered something called the "inverted mystery" when they came upon *The Singing Bones* by Richard Austin Freeman. That novel presented these young minds with a revelation in structure: the reader knows early on who the killer is. The challenge then is to see how the detective manages to figure it out. It would later become their blueprint for a historic

TV series involving a detective in a rumpled raincoat.

Television arrived as a storytelling form, and Link's family had one of the first TV sets. In an interview with the Writers Guild Foundation, he talked about how formative that was for him and Levinson. "We watched all those incredible dramas – the 'kitchen table dramas' – on *Philco Playhouse*, the *US Steel Hour*, *Kraft Theater*, *Armstrong Theater*. They were written by wonderful writers. Paddy Chayefsky, Gore Vidal, JP Miller, Bob van Scoyk...We saw that very interesting – mature – dramas could be written for television, and that is where we aimed."

Chayefsky expressed surprise at the acclaim he got for "Marty," which starred Rod Steiger in 1953 on *Philco Television Playhouse*, calling the life of a butcher from the Bronx "the most ordinary love story in the world." But a young team of budding writers recognized the power in the ordinary and it took hold in their short fiction. Levinson and Link set their stories in the commonplace of everyday life; the unremarkable day when the remarkable happens. A postal carrier on rounds. A boy unhappy at summer camp. A bank teller who gets robbed. From the start, they crafted unexceptional people delivered to exceptional tipping points, either by chance or cool reckoning, where quiet desperation becomes cool calculation.

Much like those "kitchen table dramas," the twentysomethings put emphasis on dialogue over violence. William Link's comments about writing *Columbo* come right out of their nascent fiction. He said, it was "all about no guns, no violence. Talk, good talk, good clues." Link called it "migraine country" for writers because it didn't rely on hacky devices. It was their devotion to writing character – in whatever the form – that elevated their work.

Fans of *Columbo* will enjoy hints of things to come in this collection: The bloodless murder. Identification with the killer. And – courtesy of the magicians that they were – clues fairly sprinkled in plain view. In "Shooting Script" Levinson and Link even show off their cinematic chops, putting into prose the dance of the cameras in a televised scene. That story also reveals a harbinger of the classic *Columbo* killer: a professional at the top of his field. In this case he's the TV director of an analogue of the *Arthur Godfrey Show*, replete with its redheaded, abusive host. In "The Hundred-Dollar Bird's Nest" an old doctor's murderous plan foreshadows episodes like "Murder of a Rock Star" and "Stitch in Crime." The method of dispatch was also echoed in "A Nest of Vipers," a teleplay from another iconic Levinson and Link series created with Peter S. Fischer, *Murder, She Wrote*.

"Exit Line" introduces us to an actor, Jack Russo, who is the seed for a character who appears years later in one of their movies for television, *Rehearsal for Murder*. (Keen eyes will also note the play Mr. Russo is appearing in, *Enough Rope*, was an early title of what eventually became *Columbo*.) In "One Bad Winter Day" they explore the theme of cowardice much as it later played out in another of their TV movies, 1974's acclaimed *The Execution of Private Slovik*. Same theme, different setting: instead of Europe in World War-II, it's rural Colorado where a frightened sheriff faces both a killer and retirement.

Levinson and Link's truest magic was to put us in the story. They made us feel their trademark TV series angst, a criminal's inner panic. That identification was breathtakingly rendered in "Robbery, Robbery, Robbery" when a normal Joe seizes the brass ring of chance and suffers the fate of crooked impulse. Even a surname got a dry run. "No Name, Address, Identity" features a Dr. Mannix, later recycled as the lead character in Levinson and Link's first network series creation in 1968. But, no doubt, the greatest Easter egg to be found is in the story that first appeared back in 1960 in *Alfred Hitchcock's Mystery Magazine*.

"Dear Corpus Delicti" introduces Lieutenant Fisher of the 45th Precinct. He doesn't seem like much when we first meet him. Only "a slight, insignificant little man" holding his hat near a stairway. But the role of that unremarkable policeman would expand when that short story got rewritten as the 1962 play *Prescription: Murder*, and Richard Levinson and William Link renamed Fisher, creating one of the greatest detectives of all time, Lieutenant Columbo.

In resounding understatement, "Dear Corpus Delicti" gives a glimpse of the character to come in his nonchalant lines. "It won't take long...May I come in?"

Pure Columbo.

From junior high on, these two friends, writing partners for more than forty years, practiced magic, but with no cheap tricks. They even had the confidence to reveal a trade secret in their TV Movie

Rehearsal for Murder. Levinson and Link wrote a telling line of dialogue for the playwright portrayed by Robert Preston: "I wrote a mystery...You take the audience by the hand and you lead them in the wrong direction."

We are not only their grateful audience, they respected us enough as readers and viewers to call us up as volunteers and elevate us to magician's assistant. They knew better than to give away the trick, but they always made us privy to a good glimpse of the elements. For instance, a prop, like a distinctive blue envelope with black trim, a boy's wet shoes, a thousand-dollar bill with a name on a piece of paper wrapped around it. We got a fair chance to solve the story, but somehow they always amazed us with their dazzling sleight of hand.

As you turn the page to discover these early gems, it seems right to quote the TV director in "Shooting Script" as he began each broadcast. "All right boys...let's make some magic."

Tom Straw
Connecticut – May 2021

Tom Straw published his first mystery novel, The Trigger Episode, *in 2007. Subsequently, writing as Richard Castle, he authored seven more crime novels, all of which became* New York Times Bestsellers. Buzz Killer *is Tom Straw's first book under his own name since that blockbuster Nikki Heat series. He is also an Emmy- and Writer's Guild of America-nominated TV writer and producer having written and produced* Night Court, Parker Lewis Can't Lose, Dave's World, Grace Under Fire, Cosby, Whoopi, *and* Nurse Jackie. *Currently a member of the national board of Mystery Writers of America, he lives in Connecticut, where his home is his castle.*

THE BEST-LAID SCHEMES...

William Theodore Link and Richard Leighton Levinson were born – in 1933 and 1934, respectively – and raised in a suburb of Philadelphia. Both were youthful and passionate fans of radio crime dramas, pulp magazines and magic tricks. They met in 1946 on their first day of junior high school, and it wasn't long before the two were writing together. "We began doing radio dramas on wire recorders," Levinson told Otto Penzler in a 1980 interview published in *Ellery Queen's Mystery Magazine*, "and began writing unsaleable short stories, school plays, entering writing contests."

"Don't forget the school musical," Link added.

"The first thing we ever wrote," Levinson recalled, "was a Sam Spade skit."

They spent the next forty-one years working together. In a 1983 seminar at the Museum of Broadcasting, Link explained their methods:

> One of us comes up with an idea, but both of us have to be excited by it. Then we spend a long time with the characters, structuring the piece, and finally we reach that day when we go into a study, with a typewriter, and sit down and write it. We like to do four or five pages a day. Some days are wonderful, and we do more. Some days we do less. That means the rest of the day is awful. We drive our wives crazy. But that's it. We work in the mornings and we try to do four or five pages a day, and before you know it, in five weeks the script is completed.

Levinson took it from there. "What the individual writer does in his own mind, internally, we do verbally. I say, 'Harry walks down the street,' and Bill says, 'Harry walks angrily down the street,' and

I say, 'Harry is not angry.' So it is an endless dialogue or conversation between two people."

*

Link and Levinson made their first professional sale with "Whistle While You Work," which appeared in the November 1954 issue of *EQMM*. Written while its authors were still in high school, the story was published when they were attending the Wharton Business School at the University of Pennsylvania. But a career in business wasn't what they had in mind, and the sale to *EQMM* cemented their decision to pursue the writing game.

The Golden Age of Television was in full swing. Link and Levinson broke into the field in the late 1950s, crafting episodes of *Richard Diamond, Private Detective, Michael Shayne,* and *The Third Man,* among others. "Enough Rope," written for *The Chevy Mystery Show* in 1960, featured an eccentric detective with an offbeat way of questioning his suspects, a disheveled David who brought law-breaking Goliaths to justice. Columbo was his name – Lieutenant Columbo.

Link and Levinson brought Columbo back in the 1962 stage play *Prescription: Murder* and in 1968's TV movie version. This led to a critically lauded and vastly popular series that made the raincoat-clad detective a household name. The circle was completed with a number of made-for-television specials, the last of which aired in 2003. Bert Freed was the first television incarnation of Columbo. Thomas Mitchell, best known as *It's A Wonderful Life*'s Uncle Billy, handled the role onstage. But, as the entire world knows, the part is forever wedded to the inimitable Peter Falk. Link and Levinson's collaboration with Falk is one of the all-time great fusions of writers, character and actor.

Each episode of *Columbo* followed the same pattern. Critic and novelist William L. DeAndrea described it in his *Encyclopedia Mysteriosa*: "We see someone commit what looks like the perfect crime…and then we see the seemingly bumbling detective take the perfection to pieces." As Link has pointed out, Columbo's foes are the rich and the powerful, and he attributes a portion of the show's popularity to the fact that the good lieutenant is a working-class underdog. He represents the viewer, and the viewer exults in the piece-by-piece dismantling of the villain's smug belief in his (or her) invincibility.

Columbo is, as Gwen Inhat wrote for the A.V. Club's website, "the most iconic TV detective of all time." But he's not the only crime fighter Link and Levinson brought to the small screen. Other series include *Mannix, The Bold Ones, Tenafly, Ellery Queen, Blacke's Magic,* and (with Peter S. Fischer) *Murder, She Wrote* – which introduced the world to crime-solving mystery writer Jessica Fletcher.

Murder, She Wrote was a phenomenon, but the show's success was far from a sure thing. *Murder's* stories had no sex, little violence, and featured a smart, independent older woman who, as Link said in an interview for the Archive of American Television, "wasn't bailed out by the men in the last reel." Jessica Fletcher can take care of herself. In *The Fine Art of Murder,* Margaret C. Albert offered an assessment of Ms. Fletcher's strengths: "Jessica is not an old lady. She moves comfortably through a house of prostitution, parades as a frumpy hypochondriac out to expose a phony doctor, and adroitly (and politely) upstages big-city cops who underestimate her skills."

Like Columbo, Jessica Fletcher was featured in a number of highly rated television movies after the series ended. She is, without a doubt, the second unforgettable character in Link's and Levinson's work.

Link and Levinson had a parallel career as pioneering writers / producers of television movies that dealt with racial prejudice (*My Sweet Charlie*) and, violence in the media (*The Storyteller*) and in life (*The Gun*). *That Certain Summer* was, according to the *New York Times,* "the first TV film to take a mature and non-remonstrative approach to the subject of homosexuality." *Crisis at Central High* dramatized the historical 1957 integration of a high school in Little Rock, Arkansas. *Terrorist on Trial: The United States of America vs. Salim Ajami* was a prescient look at Middle-Eastern fundamentalism and the American legal system. In 1961, FCC chair Newton N. Minow referred to television as a "vast wasteland," but Link and Levinson definitively proved that the medium was capable of great and serious things, and could be used to illuminate and educate.

It can also mystify and delight, as evidenced by a trio of Edgar-Award winning TV movies: *Murder by Natural Causes*, *Rehearsal for Murder* and *Guilty Conscience*. These are fiendishly clever dramas that put the viewer through the proverbial wringer. They exemplify the pair's appreciation of what William L. DeAndrea called "the classical aspects of the mystery story: the clues and the solutions."

Richard Levinson died of a heart attack in 1987; he was fifty-two. Link continued working on his own, developing new television series and publishing stories in *EQMM* and *Alfred Hitchcock's Mystery Magazine*. Mystery Writers of America awarded him Grand Master status in 2018, the ultimate recognition and crowning achievement of a lifetime dedicated to the genre.

William Theodore Link died on December 27, 2020 from congestive heart failure; he was eighty-seven years old. His final months were sweetened by the knowledge that – thanks to mass binge-watching due to the COVID-19 pandemic – *Columbo* had found new generations of enthusiastic viewers. Understandably: elegantly written, directed, and acted, the series offers continuing pleasure for both new and returning viewers. An additional factor played a role in the newfound appreciation for the show. With the nation in a perilous state, subjected to the psychotic whims of its corrupt so-called leaders, the knowledge that one modest, intelligent L.A. cop made sure the arrogant rich were punished for their crimes was deeply satisfying.

Artist Joe Dator's multi-panel tribute to *Columbo's* enduring appeal turned up in an October 2020 issue of *The New Yorker*. Dator's warm and witty encomium captures the affection so many of us feel for that rumpled and unassuming lieutenant. It is, in fact, something stronger than mere affection we feel.

Columbo is loved.

And so are his creators.

*

Link and Levinson brought high-quality mystery storytelling to a national and international audience and introduced millions of viewers to the pleasures of the mystery form. Their work has intrigued and entertained millions and upheld the highest standards of the craft.

It's time their short stories received some of the attention they so amply deserve.

The characters populating the fiction of Levinson and Link embody the truth of the Scottish poet Robert Burns' famous lines: "The best-laid schemes o' mice an' men / Gang aft a-gley / An' lea'e us nought but grief an' pain, / For promised joy." Time and again, desperation and desire – for money, for escape, for a bit of peace and quiet in a chaotic world – lead their characters to commit crimes. Time and again, an unexpected twist of fate crushes their dreams. Blinded by their obsessions, they step into the graves they've dug for others. Only rarely does a scheme *not* go awry, as in "Whistle While You Work," in which the hen-pecked postman Reber Shelley finally regains his long-lost *joie de vivre* by a simple sin of omission. Their other characters are not so lucky. Justice – poetic or legal – is all they get for their criminous efforts…and all they deserve.

Several of the stories are credited to "Ted Leighton," a pseudonym used by Levinson and Link when more than one of their tales appeared in a given issue of *AHMM*. (It was also the name they used when unhappy with the way a script of theirs had been realized. *Ellery Queen: Don't Look Behind You* from 1971 is Leighton's greatest claim to shame. Disheartened by the changes made to their adaptation of EQ's classic novel *Cat of Many Tails*, Levinson and Link disowned the project and gave the always-amenable Leighton the credit. In 1975 they brought a far more faithful version of Queen's work to the small screen in *Too Many Suspects*, featuring Jim Hutton as the lanky detective and David Wayne as his diminutive father. Hutton and Wayne reprised their roles in a short-lived but much-loved TV series.)

Most of the stories first appeared in *AHMM*. It's easy to see why the magazine liked their work, and why they wrote for Hitchcock's television show: these tales of small lives looking for a big pay-off are exactly the kind of stories Hitchcock offered viewers week in and week out. The portly director had some advice to offer the team. "We once had a three-hour lunch with the Master of Suspense in his bungalow at Universal," Link told Andrew McAleer.

"Writing-wise, [Hitchcock] said that when you use coincidence it must occur early in the script and never again. Always go for the big, important scenes even if they defy logic."

*

Hamlet informs us that brevity is the soul of wit; it should also be the soul of introductions. So without further ado, here are seventeen tales guaranteed to tie your stomach in knots and make your pulse race.

Joseph Goodrich
Jackson Heights, NY
April 2021

Joseph Goodrich is a playwright whose work has been produced across the United States and published by Samuel French, Playscripts, and Applause Books. Canada's Vertigo Theatre produced the world premiere of his adaptation of Ellery Queen's novel Calamity Town (2016 Calgary Theater Critics' Award for Best New Script). Panic received the 2008 Edgar Award for Best Play. He is the editor of Blood Relations: The Selected Letters of Ellery Queen, 1947-1950 and People in a Magazine: The Selected Letters of S. N. Behrman and His Editors at "The New Yorker." His fiction has appeared in Ellery Queen's Mystery Magazine, Alfred Hitchcock's Mystery Magazine, and two MWA anthologies. Unusual Suspects: Selected Non-Fiction was published in 2020. An alumnus of New Dramatists, and an active member of MWA, he is a former Calderwood Fellow at MacDowell.

FD

May 9, 1953

Dear Mr. Mills:

In answer to your letter of May 8 requesting
some information about us: We are both 19 and
attend the University of Pennsylvania. We first
met in Junior High where we found we had three
like hobbies; reading detective fiction, magic,
and wire recording. From then on we began collaborating on short stories, writing and directing
crime dramas for Cheltenham Radio Club, and staging
burlesque mystery shows. In our Senior year we
wrote and produced an original musical comedy. Its
success inspired us to consider a writing career,
but immediately dire warnings of "you'll starve!",
"it's impossible to get something published", etc.
greeted us. So, heeding these dark prophecies, we
now find ourselves students at the Wharton School
of Commerce and Finance at Penn. But even though
our ambitions have been temporarily stifled, we still
have an eye cocked on the School of Journalism.

Between classes and fraternity functions, we are
turning out monthly articles for Pennpix (U. of P.'s
humor magazine), radio scripts, detective short
stories, and plotting a tentative script for Penn's
annual "Mask and Wig" production. This summer, when
academic subjects are abandoned, we will begin work
on an original musical comedy for Syracuse University
and our first detective novel.

Recently Mr. Robert Jawer of TV Station WPTZ
(N.B.C.'s affiliated station in Philadelphia) has
asked to see samples of our work. We submitted this
material last week and are waiting to see what happens.

As things are going now, we are headed for business
careers. Of course, we still have three more years of
college and many things can happen to change our minds
in that time.

Thanking you for the interest you have taken in us,
we remain

Sincerely yours,

William Link

William Link
Richard Levinson

Pd. $135
5/26/53

ELLERY QUEEN'S MYSTERY MAGAZINE

A Mercury Publication. 570 Lexington Avenue, New York 22, N.Y.

Lawrence E. Spivak, PUBLISHER. Ellery Queen, EDITOR

May 13, 1953

        In consideration of __ONE HUNDRED AND THIRTY-FIVE__
($135.) DOLLARS, I̶,̶ __WILLIAM LINK and RICHARD LEVINSON__,
the authorş byxxxxxxxxxxxxxxxxxxxxxxxxxxxxxxxxxxxxxxxxxxx̶m̶y̶
̶a̶u̶t̶h̶o̶r̶i̶z̶e̶d̶ ̶a̶g̶e̶n̶t̶x̶ do hereby sell, transfer and assign to
Mercury Publications, Inc., publishers of ELLERY QUEEN'S
MYSTERY MAGAZINE, the first North American serial rights
and first foreign rights in the original, unpublished
story entitled __WHISTLING (our first professional short stor̶y̶)__for
publication in the various editions of ELLERY QUEEN'S
MYSTERY MAGAZINE. We agree that the right to use said
story will not be sold or assigned to any other magazine,
any newspaper, radio or television program, or book publisher prior to its publication in ELLERY QUEEN'S MYSTERY
MAGAZINE, and for six months after such publication. We
further agree not to sell this story at any time to any
other detective or suspense publication directly com-
petitive with ELLERY QUEEN'S MYSTERY MAGAZINE without the
permission of ELLERY QUEEN'S MYSTERY MAGAZINE. We grant
to Mercury Publications, Inc. an option on first book an-
thology rights which, when exercised, will call for a
payment to the authors of THIRTY-FIVE ($35) DOLLARS, plus
a pro rata share of twenty-five (25%) per cent of the
full royalty paid by any book club that selects this an-
thology.

        Mercury Publications, Inc. reserves the right to
change the title of the story, and to publish it in trans-
lations, where necessary. Mercury Publications, Inc. will
copyright the story in its own name as part of the copyright of the magazine. The authors agreeʂ that all sub-
sequent uses of this story will carry the statement that
it was first published in ELLERY QUEEN'S MYSTERY MAGAZINE.
It is understood that six months after publication,
Mercury Publications, Inc., upon request, will assign to
the undersigned authors the copyright of the above story,
subject to all the rights and privileges of Mercury
Publications, Inc. herein provided for.

WHISTLE WHILE YOU WORK

"Whistle While You Work" appeared in the November 1954 issue of *Ellery Queen's Mystery Magazine*, prefaced with these remarks from editor Frederic Dannay:

William Link and Richard Levinson are the authors of "Whistle While You Work," one of thirteen "first stories" which won special awards in EQMM's Ninth Annual Contest – last year's competition. It is the sympathetic tale of a small-town mailman, his nagging wife, and the cruel heat of Cooper, Colorado…The authors, at the time of this writing, are twenty years old, and both attend the University of Pennsylvania. They first met in Junior High School, in Philadelphia, and discovered they had three things in common: reading detective fiction, performing magic, and experimenting with wire recorders. These mutual interests led to an enduring friendship, and soon they began collaborating in their work, especially in the writing and directing of school shows. In their senior year, they wrote and produced a musical comedy, and it was so great a success that both were inspired to consider writing a career. But immediately friends and family became prophets of gloom: "You'll starve!" they warned, and "You'll never have anything published!"

Well, the boys were only human – and very young. They took heed of those fearful predictions, and as a compromise with life's eternal verities, enrolled in the Wharton School of Commerce and Finance at Penn. But between classes and fraternity frolics they continue to write together, turning out pieces for "Pennpix" (U. of P.'s humor magazine), radio scripts, and detective short stories. True, there is every indication they are headed for the world of commerce and finance, but we wouldn't be too surprised to see both of them wind up in the School of Journalism!

One thing, however, is sure: the two dire, doleful warnings were unfounded. Here are the boys actually having something published, and so far as we know neither of them has starved.

The record shows that Link and Levinson did rather well in the decades following their initial foray into the world of mystery and suspense…

*

The sun was striking along the edge of the blinded windows as Reber Shelley finished dressing. On the night table the thin hands of his alarm clock pointed to 7:20. His wife still lay asleep on the small double bed.

He had finished transferring change from an old pair of pants when a sleepy moan came from behind him. "You up already?" his wife mumbled. She looked at him from the quilted cocoon of blankets. "Seems like every morning you get up earlier."

"Go back to sleep." Shelley walked toward the kitchenette, hoping she would stay in bed. "I'll get my own breakfast, Melba," he called out to her.

There was no answer from the tiny bedroom. The man in the kitchen started the coffee percolator and poured some cereal into a chipped bowl. He lifted a window shade and gazed out on the hot pocket of the little town. Heat waves were already shimmering up from the pavements, but the surrounding mountains looked cool and remote. The mercury line in the windowsill thermometer already touched eighty-five.

Shelley grumbled to himself as he poured the coffee. He could see his thin face distorted by the chrome percolator fixtures – the cracked, sun-browned skin stretched tight under the eyes, the dull gray hair matted and uncombed.

If only she stayed in bed. If just this one morning he could get out without her coming in and ruining it.

"Looks like another hot day, Reber." She stood in the doorway, drawing a dressing-gown cord tighter about her dumpy body. He hadn't heard her footsteps on the worn carpet.

"Yeah. Hate like hell to carry the mail in weather like this."

"Makes you sick, that job, doesn't it?"

He didn't look at her, but he could feel his face getting flushed. "Please, Melba. Please don't start that again."

"I'm not starting anything again." She came around to glare at him. Her round face was hollow and without character. "Let's thrash this thing out. Right now. All your life you been a mail carrier here. Every day you lug that bag – morning after morning – and what have you got? Look at you. Fifty-four and you look over sixty."

"I can't help it," he defended himself. "I work hard."

"You listen! What have you got to show? Other people got nice homes and cars. Not us. We're still living here, but you don't care. Oh, no, not you! Up every day, put on the pack, walk down the road. Like an animal, that's what you are. They could have hired an animal to do the same job."

He raised a placating hand, but it didn't stem her flow of bitter words.

"And it's changed you too. You used to be happy, you used to whistle. I could tell you felt good 'cause you always whistled. But you don't whistle anymore."

He slipped one brown leather strap of his mailbag over one arm, not listening to her at all. She clawed at his shoulder with one hand but he shrugged it off as he opened the door. Slowly he walked down the stone steps, his wife's voice storming out into the hot morning air.

"Go on," she screamed from the doorway. "Start another day just like the rest. Just like an animal. Go on!"

Walk…walk…walk…

The road dropped steadily before him, slanting down to the dusty gray pile of stones that made up the center of town. High above, the sun had cleared the hazy rim of the mountains. His shadow was etched sharply on the hard-packed earth. Heat. Dryness. Walking. Always walking.

The post office loomed up. It was the first in the line of storefronts, a red brick building, neat and compact. He entered and said good morning to Lou Rolfe, a tall, wilted man who was the town's other postman. Pop Avery sat behind the stamp window with their two piles of mail stacked before him. "Hot day," he said.

The two carriers made a rapid assortment of the mail, then transferred it to their respective bags. They said goodbye to Avery and went outside.

Shelley watched Rolfe move off toward the opposite end of town before he heaved his bag on his shoulders. The brown pouch was like a heavy weight pressing down on his back. Ahead the road stretched past the post office and on past the five stores that comprised the row. A cloud of dust rose up and choked him as he started to walk. He coughed harshly and wiped his tearing eyes with the back of a chapped hand.

Walk.

The first stop was Tashman's grocery. Through the dirt-caked window he could see Tashman's loose, white-smocked figure bent over the produce scales. The store didn't look the same without the grocer's lanky son, who had helped his father behind the counter. The boy was now in Korea, and Shelley looked through the three letters addressed to Tashman to see if any were from his son, but there were no foreign stamps. The mailman dropped the three oblongs through the door slot and walked on.

Olsen's barbershop. Olsen was shaving an early morning customer. Above the pyramid of hair tonic bottles an electric fan purred softly. It's cool in there, thought Shelley. I could drop in for a few minutes and chat with him and stand next to his fan. But no, I'd waste time, might even get into the habit of doing it. Better drop my letters and go.

He passed the other three shops in the same mechanical procedure. Look in, think about the folks inside, slip the mail in the slot, walk on. The bag felt heavier on his back, so he shifted its position. The private homes came after the stores on his route. He followed the dirt road as the sweat began to break out on his neck and stain his shirt. Walk over the road, the dirt road. He could do it with his eye closed. Walk.

Think about something else besides the heat and Melba. Think about anything except those days. Letters. Thousands and thousands of letters all delivered by him. A never-ending chain of sealed papers that would probably stretch for miles if laid end to end. Letters of love, letters of grief, of birth, of death. *Wish you were here. Will be home in two weeks.* And telegrams. *Your son is missing in action...* All coming here to Cooper, Colorado.

A hot, dry little town (population 276). A town with one sheriff, two deputies, four firemen, and two mailmen. Letters. Letters and letterboxes. Outside each home: a stenciled metal can with a red metal flag. A red metal flag burning with the heat of the sun. Here comes the mailman. Red flag up, red flag down. Each the same. Red flag up, red flag down. Heat. Melba. Walk.

He stopped at the first house, took off his bag, and rested briefly. It was a shrunken house, resting lazily on its foundations. The second house was slick and modern, freshly painted and gleaming with glass like an aquarium. All different, but in one respect, each the same. Every one had its metal mailbox. Red flag up, red flag down...

And so the morning passed as he tramped up the climbing roads. Past playing children. Past talking housewives and friends he knew. Higher and higher on his twisting route, as if the last silver box lay somewhere in the sky. He journeyed on and the sun went with him.

Finally one house left. The realization flashed through his mind as he turned and looked down the countryside. Below stretched the homes he had left, linked in a chain of bright red flags. One house left. It sat on top of the hill against a background of mountains. Charles Bywood's house. Bywood was the wealthiest man in Cooper; he commuted every day to his mill in the North. But most important, he always gave the mailman three dollars at Christmas time.

Shelley removed the last letter from his bag and turned into the sweeping driveway. He enjoyed delivering mail to this particular house. Probably it was because the load was now gone from his back and the route was over at last. He liked to walk over the crushed white stones of the driveway and watch the circlets of spray from the spinners on the parched lawn. A slight breeze, fanning out from behind a row of trees, cooled his face. It seemed that only the rich could afford the wind. The rest of Cooper seemed trapped far below, in the dusty bowl of the valley.

This morning he could see Mrs. Bywood lying on a chaise longue on a flagged patio in the rear. The silver frames of her dark glasses glinted in the sun. Shelley had almost reached her when a gust of wind flicked the letter from his hand and floated it across the lawn. It landed beneath one of the sprinklers. The mailman swore, stooped quickly, and retrieved the letter. Fortunately, only the back was wet, as he saw at a glance. The envelope was blue, with a black border, and addressed in a queer, slanting hand-writing. Rather guiltily he wiped the envelope on his shirt and dropped it in the mailbox. Maybe it would dry, he thought, before Mrs. Bywood came for it.

Then he walked down the hill, watching the rays of the sun strike at the terraced homes. He knew the temperature must be well up in the nineties by now. His muscles ached and his neck burned. Down he walked and the town came up to meet him. At last, his route was over – and he was going home to Melba.

The next day was just as hot. His wife lashed out at him as she had done the previous morning. Everything seemed the same, yet there was a subtle change. As Shelley went into the post office, he noticed the excitement. Pop Avery did not greet him with the usual "Hot day." The old gentleman was holding court in a group of townsfolk. He turned to the other mailman.

"Hear the news, Reber?" Rolfe didn't wait for an answer. "Mrs. Bywood was murdered last night!"

Shelley was puzzled more than he was surprised or shocked. Murders didn't happen in Cooper, Colorado. Cooper wasn't the setting, it was too small, too hot, too – well, they just didn't hap-pen here. The only bit of violence he could recall happened four years ago when some kids had tossed a brick through Tashman's front window. But murder!

The mailman collected his pouch of letters and started out. The dusty street was not empty as it usually was. Small knots of people stood together, hungry for conversation. The barbershop had an overflow of customers, the bakery was full of talking wom-en. Shelley pieced together what had happened from vagrant sen-tences he heard as he progressed. Mrs. Bywood had been lured to a secluded spot near the main highway, and there she had been strangled with a silk scarf. That was all. No one knew why she had gone to the secluded spot. No one had witnessed the act. The little mailman was disturbed by the fact that he had seen her the previous afternoon. She was so healthy then, so well-tanned and healthy. And now she was dead.

There were several letters for Charles Bywood, so he trudged up the hill to the house. The sprinklers stood idly on the lawn as a dry wind rustled the blades of grass. Behind the house, on the stone patio, the chaise longue was empty. A fleet of cars, their windshields marked with stickers of Northern newspapers, was parked in the driveway. The mailman was rounding the bend of the walk when the sheriff came out with two other men and called hello to him. Shelley waved, dropped the letters in the box, and started down the hill.

It was 5:30 and he had almost reached the center of town when he made a discovery. There was still one letter in his bag, half hidden by an overlapping piece of leather. It was a blue envelope with a black border. The handwriting was unusual. Shelley looked at the address and dropped the letter in the mailbox of the modern house as he passed by.

Melba was unbearable that night. Shelley sat, head lowered, at the supper table while she taunted him about his job. He was glad when the meal finally ended and he could retreat from Melba's accusing eyes. He settled down comfortably in his favorite armchair, next to the open window, and opened the evening paper.

At eight o'clock the doorbell jangled and Melba led three of her friends into the tiny living room. The visitors bid cold "Good evenings" to the mailman, and then eagerly followed his wife into the kitchen. For a solid hour, while Shelley tried to concentrate on his paper, the four women discussed the murder. Their shrill voices seemed to grow louder as the discussion progressed and soon an argument broke out. One of the women ardently defended her conception of The Strangler, as she called him; she envisioned him as a sex fiend, a man thwarted in love, who took out his hatred on defenseless women. Melba disagreed, saying he was probably Mrs. Bywood's secret lover who had killed her in a fit of anger. The argument raged stronger, the voices welling up against the warm walls of the kitchen. Shelley, his head aching with the sound, threw down his paper and left the house.

It was quiet outside. A hot, bright moon soared above the

mountains, and there was a pulsing of crickets. A few stars hung in the sky. The mailman began walking, and his feet automatically led him over the same route he traversed every day. Houses glowed against the quiet hills, and light fingers of wind curled through the dry, sparse vegetation.

Up ahead was the modern house, gleaming in the night like a mirrored box. Shelley stood thoughtfully under a tree and stared at it. He had dropped the letter there that afternoon. Strange. There had been another letter just like that one…where had he seen it? Oh, yes, now he remembered. The one to Mrs. Bywood's home, the one that had got wet. But his thoughts were suddenly cut short. The front door of the modern house opened and the woman who lived there came out. She locked the door and moved off into the deeper shadows of the road. Shelley stood transfixed, watching her tall, lithe figure disappear beyond the brow of a hill. The little road looked empty but he felt another presence. He didn't see anyone under the hot glow of the moon, but he felt something, something close at hand. And then the feeling was gone, as if whatever had caused it had followed the woman up the road…

The next day, Shelley discovered that she had been murdered. Strangled with a silk scarf. The town was now in a virtual uproar. One murder was interesting; it had conversational value. But two murders left a strong feeling of horror. The woman who owned the modern house – her name was Kent – had been found earlier that morning in a nearby meadow. She had been a quiet soul, an elderly Latin teacher at Cooper High School. She had had few friends, but no known enemies. And yet she was found dead in a dark thicket, with the silken noose around her throat.

As Shelley made his rounds he became more and more bothered by something. Not the fact that he had probably seen her walking to her death, but by something else. He couldn't pin it down. There were too many other thoughts in his mind – mostly the result of Melba's early morning tirades. Shelley was sick of them, sick of his own existence. He walked on his rounds.

But as he walked he continued to think. He thought about Mrs. Bywood and Miss Kent. He became so engrossed that he forgot the aching agony of the bag on his back. He walked past the row of houses beyond the stores, not seeing any of them. His legs carried him on his worn route as they had done every day for the past thirty years. But the silver letterboxes remained unopened by him on this particular morning. A mailman neglecting his boxes. No red flag up, red flag down this morning. Letters. They were the key to the problem, he knew. Suddenly he took off his bag and peered into its depths. Way down at the bottom was a blue envelope: a blue envelope with the unusual handwriting and the black border. Yes, there in his own mailbag was the answer.

The letters were somehow connected with the murder! They were lures; on some excuse they got the women out of their homes to a quiet place where an unknown man with a scarf could meet them. That was it, of course! Whatever else the man wrote, he probably told his victims to bring the letters with them, and he destroyed the letters just as he destroyed the people.

Shelley paused. Yes, there was another blue envelope in his bag. And he was carrying it. No, he wasn't the murderer, but he was the carrier of death. To his mind came dim memories of the Bible he had studied in the cool cloisters of the town's church. Something about the Angel of Death swooping over... The little mailman palmed sweat off his neck. He had figured it out. And in that letter in his pouch was probably the name of the murderer. He could take it to the sheriff, he could get a small amount of fame in Cooper because of his cleverness. Maybe some of those reporters might even write him up, put the story of his life on the front pages of their Northern papers. He could sit in his chair next to the window some night and read all about himself in the paper. Think of it! For once, he would be important.

If he delivered that letter, it meant certain death to the recipient. He, Reber Shelley, was the channel through which the murderer reached out with his silk scarf. He was an assistant to the Angel of Death.

He groped in his bag, turned over the blue envelope, and saw that it was addressed to *Mrs. Melba Shelley.*

For a long minute the mailman stood still. Then he walked

quickly up the hot streets of Cooper, a small figure, sharp in the bright sunlight. He paused for only a moment when he reached his own house, then slipped the letter into his mailbox.

He hefted his bag and started back on his route. He was whistling softly. It had been a long time since he had whistled while he worked.

CHILD'S PLAY

Camp Summit drowsed in the two o'clock heat. In the cedar cabins little boys lay in their bunks, staring out through screened doors at the lawns and sleeping tennis courts. Breezes stirred in the pines, but moved off toward the tent row and the lake. The boys, dreaming of afternoon triumphs, turned over and over in their bunks, waiting for rest period to end.

Arnold came slowly up the path from the lakefront. He wore khaki shorts and a t-shirt, and his socks and sneakers were dripping wet. His round solemn face, in the open sun, was curiously white.

He entered Cabin 12 and sat down on the bunk next to the door. A boy in the back glanced up from his comic book, but said nothing. Another boy, stretched out on his bed, picked up a tennis ball and stared at the newcomer. He watched Arnold kick off his sneakers and socks and change into a new pair of loafers. "You're lucky Uncle Jack isn't here," said the boy with the tennis ball. "You'd catch it for sure if he found out you just came in. You're supposed to stay in the bunk during rest period."

Arnold switched on the Hallicrafter radio set next to his bed and moved the selector band. He slid a pair of earphones over his large ears.

"Where have you been, Arnold?" asked the boy.

Arnold moved the selector band again.

"You can hear me. Those earphones aren't *that* thick, Arnold!" He threw the tennis ball at the little boy, but it hit the bunk ledge and rolled to a stop.

"Shut up," said Arnold.

"Where have you been? On another of your expeditions?"

Arnold adjusted the earphones.

The boy who had thrown the tennis ball rolled over on his back and stared up at the raftered ceiling. "You don't know everything," he said abruptly. "There's a *lot* you don't know. There's a kid in Bunk Seven that knows three times as much as you do. And *his* father works up at Princeton. Arnold?" He looked over at the bed. "What are you listening to?"

Arnold cupped his small hands over the earphones.

"Arnold? What are you listening to?" The boy stared at Arnold for a few more minutes and then lost interest and took a comic book from his trunk. He turned away against the wall.

Arnold switched off the set and put the earphones down. He removed a key from his pocket and opened the trunk at the foot of his bed. It was a green trunk, new and unmarred by labels. Inside was a jumble of crumpled T-shirts and dirty pants; at the bottom, under some luminous white stones and the mechanism of a clock, was a sheaf of stationery. Arnold took out a piece and closed the trunk, locking it carefully. He removed a handful of pencils from his pocket and selected one with a point. Then, using the steel surface of the trunk top, he began to write in a clear, firm hand.

> Dear Mother:
> This is the third time I have written to
> you this week (and today is only Tuesday). I want
> to come home. You know that. In your last letter
> (which I received last Friday) you did not even
> refer to this subject, even though I told you about
> it in my last four letters and two postcards. You
> know why I want to leave here. Father can send
> Walter up with the car, it is only a five hour
> drive (I checked). I am quite sure that Mr.
> Whiteman will refund most of what you paid.
> Don't bother sending him a letter to find out, as
> that will waste too much time and complicate
> things. I want to come home.
> (signed) Arnold

He was folding his letter when a bugle call sounded. There was an immediate yelling and shouting, the sound of feet pounding on the lawns. Youngsters raced by outside the cabin, their white shirts flashing against the summer dazzle of the lake. The bugle stopped abruptly, and there remained only the sound of boys' voices raised in the warm wonder of afternoon.

Arnold was left alone in the cabin. He addressed an envelope, slipped the letter inside, and placed it in his back pocket. Then he turned on the Hallicrafter and adjusted the earphones. He watched a group of boys in bathing suit walking down toward the beach.

"Arnold." A man stood in the doorway. He was short and balding, with a pleasant, tanned face. A whistle dangled at the end of a blue lanyard around his neck.

"Arnold. Come on."

Arnold turned the selector band.

"It's activities period," the man said. He came in and stood looking down at the little boy. "Come on, Arnold."

"I don't feel like going."

"You have to. Look, you know what will happen if I tell Mr. Whiteman. He'll dock you your free period. You don't want that to happen, do you?"

"You don't *have* to tell him."

"Yes, I do. I let you get away with this before, but I can't this time. Now come on. You've got riflery, and Uncle Paul will be checking on you if you don't show. Arnold?"

The boy hunched his thin shoulders.

"Take those earphones off. You can hear me."

"Yes, I can."

The man wiped his sweaty neck with the front of his shirt. His nose was peeling. He sat down next to the boy on the bunk and tried a different approach. What are you listening to on that thing?"

"Radio Moscow."

"Is that so? What are they saying?"

"Lots of things."

"Like what, for example?"

"They claim we're going to have a depression."

"Do you think they're right?"

Arnold frowned and touched his smooth white cheek. "No. There are a lot of reasons why we won't. One is that –"

The man put his hand on the boy's shoulder. "Arnold, will you come with me? If you don't I'll have to tell Mr. Whiteman. Now I mean that. I'm not kidding."

Arnold thought for a moment and then removed the earphones. The cabin was quiet except for the sounds of shouting and splashing from the lake.

"Okay, Uncle Jack," Arnold said to the man. He fingered the letter in his back pocket. "I'll go if you won't tell Mr. Whiteman."

It was cool in the pine forest and the air smelled of summer leaves. A group of campers, with .22 rifles, lay stomach-down on a strip of canvas matting. Their firing sounded flat and ineffectual in the dim grove. After each round a young counselor would walk back to remove the little black and white paper targets from the rack.

Arnold sat in the shadow of a dwarf evergreen, waiting his turn with the second group of boys. He was drawing numbers with a stick in the soft earth.

"Okay. The rest of you guys." The counselor turned a red, critical face to the new group and watched them tumble down on the matting. "And cut out the talk. You can't get a decent score unless you concentrate."

Arnold pressed the heavy rifle to his shoulder. The counselor stood beside him, his black moccasins almost touching the little boy's legs.

"Now concentrate."

The others began firing. Arnold yawned, closed his left eye, and pulled the trigger. He loaded and fired six times, and each bullet sang off into the underbrush.

"What are you doing?" cried the counselor. His foot pinned Arnold's rifle to the matting. "What's wrong with you? You didn't have your barrel pointing at the target."

Arnold said nothing. He leaned his head on his elbow. The other boys stared at him.

"Didn't I teach you how to fire?" added the counselor. "You squeeze the trigger. Sque-e-eze it. And you hold your breath. Didn't I teach you that?

Arnold watched an ant cross a long gully in the matting.

"What's your name?" He waited for an answer.

"His name's Arnold," said one of the boys.

"Can't he talk for himself?"

"Can he talk?" said another boy. "You should hear him sometimes." The little boys snickered. A few threw stones into the bright sky.

The counselor bent down and tried to get Arnold's attention. "So *you're* Arnold. Well, I've been told about you."

Arnold lowered his eyes and puckered his lips as if to whistle.

"You've got the idea that you can do whatever you want around here. Well, not with me. Pick up that rifle."

Arnold watched the ant. The other boys were silent.

"I told you to pick it up," said the counselor.

Arnold looked at him. "I'm through using the rifle," he said.

"You're *what?*"

"Through using the rifle."

The other boys giggled.

"You're getting out of this period," said the counselor. "Right now. You go find Mr. Whiteman and tell him that I don't want you here with the rest of us. Tell him he'll have to reassign you to volleyball or arts and crafts. I'm certainly not going to bother with you."

Arnold got up.

"Do you hear me? Go tell Mr. Whiteman that. I'll check with him tonight to make sure you did."

Arnold turned his back and walked out of the clearing. He was on the path before the others began to talk. Then the rifles sounded again and frightened birds fluttered in the underbrush. He walked very slowly with his chin pressed down on his chest, his body swaying.

Soon he was out of the forest and standing on a grassy hill that overlooked the shining ring of beach and lake. There was a group of campers already there, including two of Arnold's bunkmates.

"Arnold," called one of the campers.

The small boy came over.

"You're supposed to know everything," said the camper. "What's going on down there?"

Arnold looked. There were three automobiles and an ambulance parked in the shimmering sand. A few state policemen were walking near the dock, and Mr. Whiteman was talking to another on the deserted beach.

"They won't let anybody down there," said the camper.

"They say we all have to go back to our bunks," cried a boy with glasses. "I think somebody was hurt."

"Did *you* hear anything?" asked the camper.

"No," said Arnold. He stood silently watching the activity on the beach and then abruptly turned in the direction of his bunk.

When he entered, the boys were waiting in line to take showers in the cramped bathroom. Uncle Jack wasn't around. Arnold opened his trunk, took out a book, and began reading. The campers were talking excitedly in the showers, and steam poured through the open canvas doorway. When they were finished they came out, wrapped in towels, and padded over to the front porch. They stood there in dripping groups, staring off through the clearing to the lake. Arnold continued to read.

Before dinner the campers usually gathered by the administration building for the lowering of the flag. Mr. Whiteman would tell them the evening's activities and read any necessary announcements. Tonight the ceremony has been called off, and the boys went directly to the dining hall from their bunks. Arnold had changed his clothes, and he strolled along the gravel path behind the others. On the steps of the old building he noticed a stone that gleamed up at him in the fading sunlight. He picked it up and placed it in his pocket.

When he got inside he went slowly over to the mail table, where all late afternoon mail was stacked according to bunkers. He shuffled through the Bunk 12 pile, but there were no letters for him. Angrily, he swept the other envelopes to the floor and went over to his table. Uncle Jack was sitting at its head, his peeling face disturbed. He still wore the same sport shirt, and there were dark perspiration stains at the armpits.

"Sit down, Arnold, you're late," he said.

Arnold took his seat. He glanced at Mr. Whiteman's table across the crowded, noisy room. The camp owner sat with three older men, and they were talking quietly. Arnold looked down at his grapefruit and attacked it with his spoon.

One of the little boys, who had been lost in thought at the other end of the table, suddenly said in a loud clear voice, "Uncle Jack. What happened to Bobby Thompson? He drowned, didn't he?"

The large room was suddenly still. Mr. Whiteman and the three men glanced up. Uncle Jack frowned and waited for the rumble of conversation to begin again before he answered. "Keep your voice down, Teddy. I can hear you."

"But what happened, Uncle Jack? He's not here for dinner tonight, and one of the guys in his bunk told me –"

The counselor interrupted him. "Bobby Thompson had an accident, that's all. Mr. Whiteman will tell you all about it in the morning."

"I'll bet he's dead," said another boy, heaping sugar on his grapefruit. "I heard they found him after rest period underneath the old docks up the lake."

Now where did you hear a thing like that?" Uncle Jack tried a tentative smile. "The way foolish rumors spread around here. You boys dream up the wildest stories."

"It is *not* a wild story," said the boy stoutly. "Why would the cops be up here if something wasn't wrong? He's dead, all right."

"Maybe he was killed or something," another camper volunteered timidly.

"It was an accident," said Uncle Jack. "A simple accident. The police always come when there's an accident. Now I don't want to hear any more about it."

"Bobby was in Bunk Nine, wasn't he?" somebody whispered to Arnold. "Uncle Paul's the head of that bunk, maybe he did it. Nobody likes Uncle Paul anyway. I wish they'd put him in jail."

Arnold shrugged and buttered a piece of bread.

Dinner progressed and the big room throbbed with high, young voices and the crash of silverware. A waiter dropped a tray and it rattled like a coin on the floor. His tables laughed and applauded. Someone near the windows began to sing, "*Oh, the Deacon went down…*" The song caught on, moving from table to table across the warm room. But the old verses failed to bring the usual enthusiasm, and the song died before it reached the head counselors' table. Mr. Whiteman got up and left the room.

Arnold ate slowly, finishing a second helping of ice cream after most of his bunkmates had been excused. Uncle Paul came over and stopped beside the table.

"Hello, Paul," said Uncle Jack, mopping his mouth with a napkin. "What's up?"

The counselor frowned. "I had a little difficulty with this boy here on the rifle range today," he said, indicating Arnold. "He was causing trouble."

"Is that true, Arnold?" asked Uncle Jack,

Arnold licked his spoon carefully.

Uncle Paul shook his head. "His attitude is uncooperative. I sent him down to talk to Whiteman. Did he go?"

"Did you, Arnold?"

"No," said the little boy.

"Why not?" snapped Uncle Paul. "I *told* you to see him."

"I don't want to talk to him," said Arnold slowly.

"You're going to have to learn, fella, that you don't always do what you want."

Uncle Jack's face grew stern. "Arnold, go over to the office and see Mr. Whiteman right now. You'll probably catch him in. Then report to me after you see him."

"I don't want to talk to him. I already told you that."

"Maybe he'd better not, at least not tonight," said Uncle Paul. "Whiteman's got enough on his mind since this afternoon. Arnold can see him tomorrow."

"No, I want him to go tonight. Whiteman wants to see him sometime this week anyway. Now you go ahead, Arnold, and no back talk."

Arnold started to say something, but the two men did not seem in the mood for arguments. He slid back his chair. "Okay," he said. "But if any Special Delivery mail comes for me tonight, let me know about it." He got up and walked over to the door.

A light burned in the office of the administration building as Arnold came up the path. The place was constructed of white wood with mildewed window flaps that could be lowered in case of rain. It sat back near the clearing at the edge of the rippled lake, and Arnold could hear the cold waters sucking against the sides of discarded rowboats. He shivered a little as the night wind whipped along the path and pressed at his thin jacket. Off in the distance, orange lights went on in the recreation hall.

Arnold pushed quietly through the screen door and stood still in the room's mild darkness. Mr. Whiteman sat behind a desk, talking on the telephone. Arnold went over to a high bookcase near a row of filing cabinets and scanned the titles. He slid out one of the books and began paging through it.

Mr. Whiteman hung up the phone and swung around in his chair. "Oh, hello, Arnold," he said. "I didn't hear you come in." He was a tall, heavy man, with a brown face and short white hair.

Arnold put the book back and approached the circle of light on the desk.

"What were you reading, son?"

"*The Psychology of Children*, by Klarmann," said the boy.

"Oh, yes. That thing's been kicking around this office for years."

"It's a new book," said Arnold. "You probably just got it this season."

Mr. Whiteman tilted back in his chair and looked at the boy. He took a pipe from a desk rack and tapped it on his palm.

"Well, sit down, son. You want a Coke or something? Some soda?"

Arnold shook his head. "I just ate a little while ago."

Mr. Whiteman packed the pipe from a small pouch and lit it. He puffed vigorously for a moment, then settled back even further in his chair. "What's the problem, Arnold? What can I do for you?"

"Uncle Paul and Uncle Jack told me to see you. Uncle Paul is mad at me because I didn't listen to him on the rifle range this afternoon."

"Well, why didn't you, son? After all, he's your instructor."

"He doesn't like me."

Mr. Whiteman laughed comfortably. "Of *course* he likes you. Why, that's downright silly, Arnold. Uncle Paul likes all the campers."

The little boy was silent.

"Now come on, Arnold. You don't actually believe that any of the counselors has anything against you. Do you?"

Arnold looked up, his small eyes momentarily alive in the glow of the desk lamp. "My mother's been writing you, hasn't she?"

"What's that?"

"She won't answer my letters because she wants to keep me here. But she's been writing to you."

Mr. Whiteman expelled a long sigh. He pressed his fingertips against the edge of the desk. "Maybe we'd better have a real talk, eh, son? Now I'm going to level with you, and I expect you to be honest with me. Your mother *has* written to me. She said that you're not happy here. Is that true?"

"Yes."

"Well, why not, Arnold? You're here for a vacation, to have a good time. Why don't you like it?"

Arnold compressed his lip and remained silent.

"Is it because the other boys don't understand you? Is that it? Frankly, son, we would have put you into an advanced bunk, but we didn't think you'd enjoy yourself there."

Arnold toyed with the zipper on his jacket, sliding it up and down.

"I'm not going to lie to you, Arnold. I've been checking with your counselor and some of the campers. I understand that you're being given a rough time. I heard that someone cut all the strings off your tennis racket."

Arnold nodded.

"And I also know that someone stole a tube from your radio set."

"I got it back." The boy's thin fingers snapped the zipper along its grooved track.

"That's not the point. If you're being bothered, I want to know about it. You should have come and told me these things." Mr. Whiteman's pipe had gone out and he relit it impatiently. "Now who's behind this, Arnold? Are they boys in your bunk?"

"No."

"How many are there? I can dock them free period if they give you any more trouble."

"Only one boy's been bothering me, and you don't have to do anything."

"Look, Arnold," said Mr. Whiteman earnestly, "I'm not asking you to tell tales or anything. I just want to make things better for you. Your mother's been very concerned about your welfare, and I want to be able to tell her that you're getting along."

"Can I have a Coke now?" asked Arnold.

Mr. Whiteman frowned and went over to a small refrigerator. He removed a bottle, opened it, and handed it to Arnold. Then he sat down, rather wearily. "Now I'd like to know the name of the boy who's been picking on you. Arnold?"

Arnold wiped off the top of the bottle and drank the Coke slowly.

"Tell me, Arnold."

"Okay. It was Bobby Thompson."

Mr. Whiteman paled. "Did you say…Bobby Thompson was the boy who was giving you trouble?"

"Yes."

Mr. Whiteman stood up very carefully and moved around the desk. He pulled on his coat. "I want you to stay here for a few minutes, Arnold." His voice was uneven. "I want you to stay right here. Promise me that. I just have to see somebody for a minute. Promise me you'll wait here for me."

Arnold put the bottle on the floor. "Okay," he said.

"Read that book you were looking at. I'll be right back. All right?" He went over to the door and looked back at the boy. Then he left. Arnold heard him begin to run as soon as he reached the gravel path.

The little boy stood up. He wandered around the room, his hands in his pockets, then went over to the desk. He sat down in Mr. Whiteman's chair, opened a drawer, and took out some stationery. He uncapped a fountain pen and began to write on the creamy paper.

Dear Mother:

This is the last time I'm going to write unless I hear from you. I want to come home…

SHOOTING SCRIPT

The microphone, hung at the end of the long, pole-like boom, was poised overhead. It followed, prying, as the man walked up the path and rang the bell. Camera one moved in behind his back for an over the shoulder shot. When the woman opened the door, the camera held long enough for an establishing close-up of her face. Blonde, smoke-like hair, disciplined back into an austere bun. A smile of recognition. Blue, knowing eyes.

"Come in," she said. "He's at work."

The man entered, closing the door behind him. There was a slow dissolve from camera one to camera two inside. Boom two picked them up as they talked their way down the foyer and into the living room. When they sat on the couch and kissed each other, the camera dollied in close.

"When will he be back?" asked the man.

"Late. We have plenty of time."

Their voices hit the tilted microphone, ran through a complex of wires, and emerged in the control room. The audio man, fingers on the dials, boosted them, calmed them, toned them into perfect electric signals for broadcasting.

Camera one's tally light flashed on outside the house. It showed another man coming up the walk. This man's face was grim, his stride quick. He jammed a key into the front door, threw it open, and stalked down the foyer.

Camera two showed the two breaking their kiss at the sudden pound of footsteps. The woman, startled, tried to get up, but she was precariously balanced and fell softly back onto the couch.

Camera three, inactive until now, showed the living room doorway. The man who'd entered the house came over the threshold and stopped.

"Al —" the woman said. "Listen, I —"

Al reached into his pocket and took out a gun.

"Hey, look –" said the man on the couch. His face was in shadow.

Al fired at the two of them, emptying the gun. The mike boom raised a fraction so the sound wouldn't harm its delicate membranes.

Al watched, as did camera three, while the woman and the man slumped forward from the couch. He dropped the gun on the floor and brought his hand up to his face.

"My God," he said. "Oh, my God."

Then, while he stood there, the lights of all three cameras blinked on. The machines rolled forward on their rubber wheels, pulling their trail of cables behind them. He saw that no one was running them, that they were motivating themselves. Ponderously, they pushed forward. The long, eight-inch lenses aimed at him like snouts. He glanced over his shoulder, suddenly frantic, and started to back away, but the mike boom dipped down and stopped him. Then all the lights—bright, burning Kliegs and small baby spots—twisted on their racks and beat their brilliance on him. The camera rolled, the mike boom swayed, the lights glared. He fell down, screaming. The collision was merciful because it brought a warm darkness.

It was, of course, the same dream Al Standish had been having all week. The repetition, however, did not accustom him to it. Today, he burst from sleep like a swimmer from water, just as he had the previous mornings. And when he shaved, his hand was uncontrollable. The razor cut through the lather smoothly; then his hand twitched and a small cut, bleeding, appeared on the side of his face. He frowned and patched the cut.

When he came down for breakfast, Carol could tell he'd had the dream. "Again?" she said.

"Yeah. That's the fifth straight night. Damn thing doesn't change a bit."

"Dear, why don't you tell me what it's about?" She ran lazy fingers through her blonde hair, tightening the plastic clip that held the bun in place.

Standish sucked at his coffee. "It's not important. And it isn't the dream that bothers me; it's the way I dream it. Like a blasted television show."

"You need a vacation," Carol said. "It's as simple as that."

"I know, but try telling that to Merrick." He shook his head. "You know, I've heard about things like this happening to television directors. When they dream they see cameras and close-ups – just as if they're directing the dream from the control room. It's like being in a hall of mirrors."

"It's strange, though, that it should be the same one every night. I mean, I can understand your dreaming from a television point of view. After all, you're a television director. But if the, well, *story* of the dream is always the same, there doesn't seem to be any explanation for that, does there?"

"No, I guess not." He got up.

"Am I in it?" she asked.

"What?"

"Your dream. Am I in it?"

"No," he said uncomfortably.

"Well, it'll go away. Take a pill tonight."

He walked through the living room and down the foyer to the door. There, mechanically, she kissed him.

The KCAB-TV studios were five miles from his house, a ten-minute drive if the lights were with him. They rose in freshly washed glass and new white stone from behind a protective border of hedging. Above the revolving entrance door there were plastic replicas of the station's call letters, each one three feet high and colored by imbedded lights. An American flag flared at the end of a flagpole on the front lawn.

Standish wheeled his car into the back parking area and got out. He walked quickly to the heavy, soundproofed doors of Studio Three and went in, conscious that he was late.

The crew was already setting up in the areas reserved for *The Red Holliday Show*. Babitz was up on the catwalk, pounding at the lights and aiming them. Lederer was tapping the microphones. Rowe, the new chief, had started the cameras warming up. They all glanced at Standish when he opened the back door to enter, letting unaccustomed sunlight flood the concrete studio floor.

"Morning," said Standish. "Sorry I'm late."

Red Holliday stood in a corner applying makeup. His boyish face, reflected from a small mirror, frowned at Standish. "The show goes on at the same time, Al. When you're late we have to cut down on rehearsals."

Standish didn't like Red Holliday. Merrick had given him the show to direct as a last resort, when two other directors had walked off it in disgust. "You can handle him, Al," Merrick had said. "Sure, he's tough to get along with, but he pulls them in. See what you can do, huh? It's the best morning show we've got. And the most sponsors."

During the first few weeks Standish had made an all-out effort to become friendly with Holliday. He had discussed technical problems with him. He had conceded minor and frequently major points. He had even taken him home for dinner several times. Holliday was not married. He would smile at Standish's wife. "Carol," he would say, "you have no idea how much a good home cooked dinner means to me. Your husband's a lucky man." Then he would smile the patented Red Holliday smile.

It had worked well for a few months. Then, as the other directors had predicted, their relationship ground to a halt. Once given the chance, Holliday had been too demanding. He took to directing from the floor, waving the cameras in closer or criticizing the lighting effects Standish had worked out with Babitz.

This morning, while applying makeup, he called up to the catwalk. "Hey, Earl, why don't you kill that light this morning? It washed me out yesterday. Use a smaller one."

Standish went over to him. "Red, there was a reason for that. You don't show up under a smaller one. Check the monitor."

Holliday bowed. "I hear and I obey. Although sometimes, Al, I don't see how you can cover all the details, coming in late like this."

"Ten minutes, Red. I was ten minutes late."

"Easy," Holliday said, smiling. "Just kidding around."

Babitz called from the catwalk. "You want this thing on or off, Al?"

"Leave it on," said Standish. "We'll check it after the show if there's any washout."

Holliday, grinning, went off to have cue cards made, while Standish conferred with the floor men. There were not many problems to iron out. For Standish *The Red Holliday Show*, with the exception of its star, was an easy production. It was frankly geared for the housewives of the city and slotted for a time between their breakfast and their ironing. The fact that it was across the boards, running a half hour every morning, five days a week, built up what Merrick liked to call "habit viewing." The show featured a young girl singer, a young male harmonica player, and between them, around them, talking into their acts and joking with them, was Red Holliday. Standish did not particularly like the show. He preferred the new shows he directed later in the day. These required mere technical facility on his part; there was never any temperament involved.

Standish mounted to the control room. "Okay, people," he said over the loudspeaker system, "stand by for rehearsal."

For the next half hour, he worked over the simple mechanics of camera motion. The control room, a long booth with a glass face showing the studio floor, was isolated, and in its seclusion he felt removed from the demands and problems of the people below. Directly above the glass in front of him was a line of monitors that presented the picture each camera was taking. He had only to press a button to select the one he wanted for broadcasting.

With a corner of his mind he made the proper picture choice; his finger pressed the proper button. The major part of his thoughts, however, rambled. The big camera below, trucking and braking, reminded him of his dream. He felt, somehow, like a man in an aquarium, watching a form of life with which he had no connection. The camera rolled, the lights pulsed, and he saw himself in his living room again. The flicker of the spread monitors lulled him; he watched them through half-closed eyes.

Once more he saw himself walking down his foyer. Once more an imaginary camera focused on two lovers embracing on a couch. His wife was lovely. She kissed the stranger with an open-mouthed eagerness that she had not given to him in years. Standish strained from his director-participant position in the fantasy to see the face of her companion. He willed the camera closer. But the man's face was in shadow, just as it always was. Then his vision of himself came into the living room and reached for the gun in its pocket…

"Five minutes!"

The voice of the stage manager on the floor broke through the control room's loudspeakers. Standish, alerted by the sound, rubbed his eyes and glanced at the large wall clock. The red hand swept in its orbit, changing in each revolution to keep an exact degree of time. Babitz came into the control room and sat at his lighting panel. Lederer moved into the audio niche. Rowe, after last minute checking on the floor, came up and eased himself into his chair beside Standish.

"All right, boys," said Standish, as he did every morning, "let's make magic."

They regarded him vacantly and turned to their controls.

Standish, with one eye on the clock, tilted his headset microphone toward his mouth. "Stand by," he said. The bustle below him subsided as people moved into their opening positions. Red Holliday sat down behind his desk and faced camera one. He moistened his lips and smiled. The female vocalist waited in her set, standing before a gauze scrim that bellowed in the wind from two fans. The harmonica player sat on a stool near the mike boom, dully looking at his instrument.

The second hand touched twelve.

"Here we go," said Standish. "Spin the theme. Coming out of slide. Steady one. Cue Holliday. One!" He activated camera one, and Holliday's smile lit the row of monitors in front of him.

"Good morning, Mom," said Red Holliday. "Here's another Red Holliday gabfest for you. So why don't you just sit down and finish that cup of coffee and give a listen? Huh? How about it?"

The show went as it always did, without crisis or mishap. Long ago, Standish had found that he could direct without becoming involved, much as the driver of a car could shift gears and turn corners while engaged in conversation. His fingers darted over the control board while he thought about the problems that had crept up over the past few months. His job, and he couldn't deny it any longer, bored him. He needed a rest, a journey to blue lakes and warm suns. And there was that most troublesome of feelings, the vague impression that Carol was drawing away from him. That, of course, was the root of the dream. But why, he wondered, carefully dissolving from camera one to camera two, did the dream involve another man? Carol's recent aloofness did not imply infidelity. And would he be jealous enough to use a gun if he discovered proof of unfaithfulness? Of course not. Besides, he didn't have a gun.

Then the thought came to him that the night watchman had a gun. It was kept in a flimsy locker in the basement, secured by a lock of doubtful strength.

Feeling foolish, Standish gave himself to the monitors. The clock wound away the segments of the show; Red Holliday was whimsical in triplicate; the girl sang and the boy played his harmonica, and eventually Standish said into his headset, "Give them thirty."

"Well, that about does it for this morning," said Holliday, one eye on the floorman's cue. "We'll all be seein' you tomorrow, and we got some real special things for you. Okay? Take care of yourself and have a good day."

"Spin it," said Standish, and the music sounded from the audio corner. "Going to black." He leaned over and yelled into the intercom on his panel that led to the master control room, "It's all yours, master." Then the on-air monitor in front of him lit up with the station's call letters. "This is KCAB," said a voice, "bringing you the best in news and entertainment."

Standish leaned back and took off his headset. He lit a cigarette. The three engineers, with a great deal of shuffling and snapping of switches, left the control room. Below, the floor cleared rapidly as the stagehands struck parts of the sets and the cameramen headed for the station commissary for coffee.

Standish was always mildly surprised by the speed with which the studio emptied itself. First the show would be on the air – everyone vitally concerned with its smooth facilitation – then within seconds after it finished the lights would go out, the cables would be braided, and the large room would be stark and desolate. He sat now in the control room, watching the process. The air seemed warmer with the discharge of his energy and he felt sleepy. His next show was not for two hours, and the studio would be empty until the afternoon. He leaned back in his swivel chair, pushed his cigarette into an ashtray, and dozed off.

It was a surface sleep, not the real thing, and he was able to dream what he wished. There was Carol, as she had looked five years ago on a Maine honeymoon, bundled up and flushed under bright autumn trees. And there was Carol, as she looked every morning now, oddly remote, sidestepping carefully all moments of tenderness.

This last thought woke Standish completely and he frowned. He was perspiring, and his shirt was stuck to his back. Below him, on the floor, someone stood in a shadowed corner, talking on a telephone. Aside from that one dim person, the studio was empty. Standish noticed idly that the mike boom, left by the crew, hung over the telephoner's head. Just as idly, he glanced at the audio panel and its switches. Smiling under a sudden compulsion of mischief, he turned on the boom.

"…able to get out of here in a few minutes. Soon as I take this makeup off."

The voice was Red Holliday's. Standish was about to turn off the switch, but he paused.

"Okay, fine. The last news show is at four. He probably won't be home until four-thirty. Uh-huh. Call him and tell him you'll be out most of the afternoon so he doesn't phone. That's right. I'll be over in twenty minutes…Sure, hon, of course." There was an amplified click as the phone was cradled.

Standish watched as Holliday crossed under the racks of dead lights and left the studio by a side door. Then he turned off the microphone. He sat thinking.

"Al?" The voice came from the intercom box to master control. "Al, you up in studio three's control room?"

"Yes."

"You're being paged."

"Thank you."

Standish picked up the phone. "Hello?"

"Who is this, please?" said the voice of the station operator.

"Al Standish."

"Oh. Just a minute, Mr. Standish, I have a call for you."

There was a pause, then Carol's voice. "Is that you, Al?"

"Yes."

"I tried to call you in your office, dear, but you weren't there."

"I'm in the control room."

"I watched the show," she said.

"Did you?"

"Yes. Very good. You had some nice shots of the singer. And Red was rather funny. Nice show."

"Thank you."

"The reason I called, I'll be out shopping all afternoon. I won't be back until a little before you get home. When are you through, by the way?"

"Four."

"All right. I'll see you then. Maybe we can go out for dinner. Bye."

"Goodbye."

Standish hung up and left the control room. He walked across the studio floor and out into the corridor. Two secretaries, hugging schedules, said good morning to him. Miss Jason, Merrick's secretary, said Merrick wanted to see him when he had time. And one of the studio guides, in answer to his question, said that Red Holliday had just left.

He parked the car and walked up the front path. Holliday's red convertible was parked down block, half obscured by a neighbor's hedges. Standish opened the door quietly and moved down the short foyer, his feet careful on the soft carpet.

The high-fidelity set was on in the living room and he heard the sound of glasses. When he entered, the two of them stared. His wife tried to get to her feet, but slipped back on the couch.

"Al –"

Holliday set down his glass on the coffee table and stood up. "I guess this looks kind of funny, doesn't it?" he said, half smiling. "Believe me, Al, it's not what you think. I just came over to..." His voice ran down. He could not think of anything.

Standish took the gun out of his pocket.

"Hey, now look –" Holliday began.

Standish fired twice. Then he turned the gun on his wife. She was trying to get to her feet when he shot her.

After they had both fallen, Standish looked around to see if there was a mike boom above him, or carefully positioned cameras. He sat down in a chair and let the gun drop to the rug. Then he waited patiently for the darkness.

When he awoke he smiled because it occurred to him that the dream had changed. This time no cameras, no hall of mirrors viewpoint. This time just a straight and simple dream. Since some of the basic elements had changed, perhaps it would go away. He would go down to breakfast and tell Carol.

He looked around the room, puzzled. He must still be asleep. Holiday and his wife, lifeless, lay beside each other. The gun was on the rug. Standish felt a little bewildered; his thoughts were clouded. He tried to think, but the pounding on the front door disturbed him.

He decided he'd go and open it and get rid of whoever it was. Then he could sit down and wait to wake up.

SUDDENLY, THERE WAS MRS. KEMP

One month after Walt Hannis killed his wife he received a telephone call from the woman who lived in the upstairs apartment. It was late in the day and he had just returned from work. His feet, swollen, were giving him a great deal of pain.

The phone began to ring as he was pulling off his shoes. He scowled at it, then went over to pick it up.

"Yes?"

"Mr. Hannis? This is Mrs. Kemp."

The name meant nothing to him. "What can I do for you, Mrs. Kemp?"

"Surely you remember me," said the woman. "I live in Eight-B, the apartment right over yours. I was at the funeral."

Vaguely, Hannis remembered a widow who had recently moved into the building, a woman addicted to kimonos and bohemian clothes. She had come to his wife's funeral, crying noisily over the open coffin, and he had occasionally seen her taking the sun in the apartment courtyard. "Yes, I know who you are. What do you want?"

"I was just wondering if you could come up for a few minutes. It's really very important, and I won't keep you long."

"Well, I just got home from work, and I – "

"Believe me, Mr. Hannis, it's urgent. Just for a few minutes."

Hannis told her he'd be up shortly. He hung up and filled a glass with tap water. The apartment, small and confining, depressed him. It was good to get out of there in the mornings, away from the yellow wallpaper and the brass-legged bed in which he spent so many bad nights. The dream about Rose was still with him, about how she had looked just before she fell. Hannis finished the water, put the glass in the sink, and laced his shoes.

The door to apartment Eight-B stood open and Mrs. Kemp was just inside it, watching him climbing the stairs. "Come in," she said.

Hannis was puzzled. He followed her into the room. It was a duplicate of his own, but heavily decorated with beads, doilies, and ceramic trays and plates. The walls were hung with Oriental fabrics and prints that had grown old and stiff.

"Why don't I make some tea," said Mrs. Kemp.

"Okay."

He sat down, watching her move into an alcove and light a flame under a heavy copper kettle. She wasn't a bad-looking woman for her age, he decided. The body was full under the pink silk house-dress. The neck, however, was heavy with loose flesh and powdered wrinkles. He watched her, waiting for her to say something.

"You certainly get up early," she said suddenly.

"It's my job," Hannis replied. "Six every morning."

"I can hear you moving around through the floor. You usually wake me."

"Well – I don't mean to – "

"Of course not," she said. It's just that the walls and floors are so thin." She turned from the stove and smiled at him. "A body can hear almost everything that goes on."

Walt nodded, feeling uneasy. Beside him, in a wire cage, was a small parakeet.

"I hope you take your tea strong," said Mrs. Kemp. "The way some people drink it, it's like water." She took two cups from a shelf above the sink and set them on the stove. "It must be hard getting up by yourself in the mornings," she said. "I mean, now that Rose isn't – well, isn't here." Her blue lashes fluttered in sympathy.

"Yeah, it is rather hard."

"Terrible thing about your wife," she said slowly. "They decided it was suicide at the inquest, didn't they? She jumped right before you came home from work."

"That's right," said Hannis uncomfortably. He shifted around in his chair and folded his legs.

Mrs. Kemp came into the room with the tea and gave a cup to Hannis. "Drink it while it's good and hot," she said, sipping her own. She ran a finger along the parakeet's cage. "You and your wife always argued a lot, didn't you? I could hear it from up here. Fighting and quarreling."

"So we didn't get along. Maybe that's why she killed herself. I don't know." He put down the cup. "And I don't think it's any of your – "

"Of course not," she said, smiling. "But when you're a lonely woman and you have nothing to do but clean an apartment, I suppose it's a bad habit you get into, listening and watching other people."

"Frankly, Mrs. Kemp – "

"You'd be surprised what I see from my window. Really. The neighbors across the courtyard, the people out on the street. Why just last month, when I was leaning out to clean the windows, I found I could see the window of your apartment."

Hannis got up. "I don't see any point to this."

"Sit down, Mr. Hannis," she said. Her voice was cool and even. Then she chuckled. "Your tea is getting cold. You'd better drink it."

He slumped back into his seat, watching her carefully.

"As I was saying, I found that I could see your window. And do you know, I actually saw your wife fall. Isn't that interesting?"

Hannis remained silent.

"Actually," she continued, "it was a horrible thing. Lord knows, I can still hear her screaming in my sleep. But you wouldn't know about the scream, would you? You weren't home at the time."

"All right," said Hannis. "Just what the hell are you getting at?"

The woman clucked at the parakeet. Then she finished her tea, studying Hannis over the rim of the cup. "You were home, Mr. Hannis," she said. "I saw you. And your wife didn't jump; you pushed her."

Hannis had been expecting it. He remained calm. But his palms on the arms of the chair were sweating. "I don't know what you're talking about, Mrs. Kemp."

It seemed as if Mrs. Kemp hadn't heard him. She went on talking, her fingers sliding up and down one of the bars of the birdcage. "I'm sure you can imagine my surprise," she said. "Here I am, leaning out to clean my windows, and I see two people struggling by your window. Then the man pushes the woman and she falls. Well, of course, I'm not the type to involve myself in other people's affairs, so I've been very quiet about it. I wouldn't want to cause anybody any trouble." She bent down over the cage. "But then, I'm an honest woman, aren't I, Billy?" The parakeet raised its blue head. "Sure I am. Billy knows. But it costs money to keep a lady honest. Don't you think so, Mr. Hannis? There's the room rent and food — "

"This is crazy!" Hannis said, his voice shaking. "Why – you're trying to blackmail me."

"—clothes and doctor's bills," said Mrs. Kemp. "Terrible how much money you spend these days. Now isn't it possible that you could give me, well, a little help? I mean, it's not asking too much; you have a job."

"I'm getting out of here," said Hannis. He stood up and started for the door. "I had nothing to do with it. You can't prove a thing."

Mrs. Kemp lifted the telephone receiver and put a finger in the dial. "I'm sure you weren't involved, Mr. Hannis. It was probably my imagination. But I do think I should let the police know about it. As a matter of civic responsibility." She began to dial.

Hannis strode to the telephone and pressed the cut-off bar. He looked at her. "All right," he said. "What do you want?"

Things, Walt Hannis decided, were worse than they had been before. Rose might just as well still be alive, still shouting and clawing at him, still nagging at everything he did. The wonderful freedom following her "accident" – and Hannis still chose to think of it an accident – was gone now. Rose had been replaced by Mrs. Kemp, and the latter was equally as unbearable. And more dangerous.

The monotony of his job added to his discomfort. He walked the hot, treeless blocks of the city, his mind never far from his problem. It was not the money. Mrs. Kemp only wanted twenty-five dollars a week. But it was the idea of what she had seen, of what her spoken word to the wrong person could do to him. And the twenty-five dollars might increase to thirty, to forty, to whatever she felt she needed.

To Hannis, there didn't seem to be a stopping point. He would be linked with her as long as she lived. Then it came to him, just as it had with Rose, that her life did not have to continue. That he, with his hands and with the will to use them, could solve the problem quite simply. And quite permanently.

Mrs. Kemp called him at the end of the week. Hannis was eating a sullen meal in his apartment when the telephone rang. He answered it.

"Hello," she said. "Just wanted to know when I can expect my first present."

"In a few days," Hannis growled. "Don't get too anxious."

Her laugh, over the phone, was not melodic. "I think we should set up a regular schedule," she said. "From now on, let's make it Friday of every week. You can drop it in my mailbox downstairs."

"I'll bring it up," he said.

"Very well. But I think there's something I should clear up, Mr. Hannis. A few days ago I wrote down everything I know about your wife's death."

"What! Damn it, you shouldn't have done that! If anybody sees —"

"No one will see it. I sealed it in a letter and gave it to a friend. If anything happens to me she has instructions to mail it immediately."

"You're really being careful, aren't you?"

"Well, Mr. Hannis, I wouldn't want to fall from a window. If you know what I mean. The letter, I think, is rather good protection."

Hannis slammed the receiver down in reply. The stupid woman thought she had him trapped. She had taken the obvious precaution of a written letter containing the evidence. And she thought that would keep her from harm, did she? Hannis smiled. Then he sat down at the table, his appetite aroused, and finished his supper.

Later, with a bottle of wine, he lay slumped in a chair, staring at the dim yellow walls. After the wine took effect, he could see Rose's face in a shadowed pane of the window. He poured another glass and Mrs. Kemp's face wavered over Rose's. Poor old widow, he thought, do you really think your letter can stop me?

There were a few things to be worked out, of course. Hannis realized that two deaths in the same building within a short span of time might be viewed with suspicion by the authorities. As to method, it would be another "accident" – not from a high place, but perhaps…

He had her death all worked out before he went to bed that evening.

There was no one in the hallway. Hannis knocked on the door, mindful of the way noise carried in the cramped building. He could hear bedsprings from inside her room and then the soft pad of her feet on the floor. Mrs. Kemp opened the door. She looked at him for a moment. The robe she had thrown over her shoulders was not quite belted.

"I didn't mean to wake you," he said. "But I owe you something."

"Are you insane? It's six o'clock in the morning." In the pale light of the hallway her face, without makeup, seemed swollen.

"I have to get to work," he said, brushing roughly past her into the room.

She closed the door and followed after him. "This isn't funny," she said. "The next time you'll leave it downstairs in my box."

"The next time?" said Hannis. He smiled.

She tightened the robe. "All right, give it to me and get out of here."

Hannis walked into the little alcove and studied the stove, just like the one in his apartment, the burners on top and a gas oven. He opened the door and turned on the gas.

"What are you doing?" she said.

Hannis took a handkerchief from his pocket and began knotting it around his fist.

"Now look," she said, "turn off the oven. You'll fill this place with gas."

"You know," Hannis said conversationally, "there's really no reason why I shouldn't kill you, is there?"

She merely seemed impatient. "Will you turn off that oven? Just turn it off, give me my money, and get out of here."

"You don't seem very frightened," he said.

"Frightened?" She laughed. "You're the one who should be

frightened. Do you think I'm bluffing about that letter? Do you think my friend won't send it?"

"I don't think you're bluffing," said Hannis. "But it doesn't matter." He tied the ends of the handkerchief around his fist. For a moment he felt sorry for her. Then he started toward her.

Her dull eyes flickered. She took a step back. "I've got a letter," she said. "I'm telling you, if anything happens to me —"

He hit her, almost lightly, on the side of her face. She fell into his waiting arms and he inspected her skin. His fist, with the handkerchief, had not left a mar.

Hannis brought a chair from the living room and set it before the stove. He put Mrs. Kemp into the chair and rested her head inside the oven. The kitchen window was open a few inches and he closed it.

The problem of a suicide note had bothered him, but he had eventually decided it would not be necessary. The neighbors would tell the police she was a widow, and probably didn't have much to live for.

On his way out of the apartment, he passed the parakeet in its cage. He wondered, idly, if it would also die from the gas fumes. Then he went into the hallway and closed the door behind him.

The next morning the mailman delivered his usual large stack of mail to the district attorney's office.

"Lord, it seems we get more each day," one of the secretaries complained to the carrier. "Why don't you keep a few and save us some work?"

"I might do that," said Walt Hannis. He shifted his heavy mail pouch and went out into the summer street.

OPERATION STAYING-ALIVE

Staff Sergeant Benny Keller sat in the barracks day room reading the same magazine endlessly. He was a small, nervous man, a veteran of Bastogne and Korea. The sergeant stripes had always pleased him; he was perfectly satisfied with the rank. His goals, simply and clearly defined, were to make sure the barracks stayed clean (No butts in the latrines, men), to keep his full-field pack rolled in a seamless tube, and to alienate no one from battalion commander to battalion goof-off. The enlisted men, sensing his hesitancy, had affectionately named him "Old Play-It-Safe."

Sergeant Keller put down the magazine and looked at his watch. It was almost one o'clock in the morning. Like most weekend nights, the enlisted men were staggering back from Munich bars and strip-joints, their eyes glazed, their voices loud. Sergeant Keller went out on the town rarely; when he did, he took a quiet beer in a country *gasthaus* or visited a pudgy-armed seamstress he had met in his first month overseas. But Sergeant Keller was content to remain in the barracks on wild Saturday nights, making sure his men got back before curfew.

Keller stood up and walked to the fuse box. He checked his watch again to be sure, then switched off all the hundred-watt lights in the day room. He bent over the pool table and sank a few balls that clicked and glimmered in the cold starlight. The outer door banged open suddenly and a weaving trio entered, their breaths smoking white in the fresh blast of air. They edged, laughing along the pool table, rocking and sliding. "Put on the damn lights, Keller," one of them said.

"Can't. It's almost oh-one-hundred, men."

"Ol' Play-It-Safe," someone snickered.

Keller smiled. He watched them tumble into the change of quarters' room to sign in. A few minutes later they were talking in the barracks, preparing for sleep.

Sergeant Keller replaced the cue-stick in its stand and stared through the window. There were deep, blue drifts of snow outside; the mess hall shone like an ice-cube. Keller lit his pipe and waited. He knew there was one E.M. missing: Pete Cobb, a tall, morose man who worked in the battalion message center. He had never liked Cobb. The man was a shifty-eyed shirker who always escaped morning clean up by claiming work in the message center.

A shadow moved by the mess hall. Keller strained his eyes and saw a tall, wobbling figure, sloshing its feet in the snow. Looks like Cobb, Keller thought. It better be. I wouldn't want to have to report him.

He waited, puffing rapidly on his pipe, cracking his knuckles in the growing chill of the big room.

The outer door opened and the figure came in. It bent over the radiator for a moment, seeking the remaining warmth. It was breathing heavily, hoarsely.

"That you, Cobb?" Keller asked.

The figure nodded and took a few steps forward. Keller made out Cobb's large, blunt face, bruised with shadows.

"You're the last one. You just made it in time."

Cobb grunted.

"What's wrong? You're out of breath."

"I was runnin'. Hadda make curfew."

Keller studied him. "You look like you been in a fight or something."

Cobb was silent. He looked around the room, shoved his big hands into his pockets.

"Well, get to bed. I wouldn't want the O.D. come checkin' around and findin' you still up."

Wordlessly, Cobb turned and went down the long corridor. Keller watched him stop and turn into the shower room. A moment later he heard the stinging splash of water on the tile floor. What the hell's he takin' a shower for? Keller thought. Suppose the O.D. comes over?

Sergeant Keller closed the day room door behind him and walked softly down the dark corridor. Steam was pouring from the open shower room. He stopped in the doorway and looked in.

Cobb, naked, stood in one of the stalls, soaping his furred flanks.

"You were in a fight, weren't you?" said Keller.

"Cobb looked at him, his face perfectly blank. Then he turned back into the rushing water.

Keller shrugged and walked the rest of the corridor to his room.

There were men shouting and whistles blowing. The lights were on. Sergeant Keller squirmed to a sitting position in his bed. It was dark outside the window of his room and the C.Q., a small, fat boy, stood in the doorway. "Sarge?" he said.

"What's going on?" Keller asked. "What time is it?"

"Just got a call from the O.D.," the C.Q. said. "We gotta get the company out on the street."

Keller began pulling on his field trousers. "Why?"

"Don't know, Sarge. He just rang up and said to get 'em out."

Keller fumbled into a woolen shirt and then went out to the corridor. Young soldiers came sleepily from the squad room, pulling on articles of clothing. "What cooks, Sarge?" "Where's the fire?" "It's three o'clock in the mornin'!"

"Fall out in the company street," Keller said. "On the double."

He marched down the middle aisle of the squad room, calling at huddled forms wrapped in khaki blankets, prodding half-asleep bodies sitting motionless on the edges of beds. "Let's go, men! Fall out! Shake it!"

Cobb was still under his blanket at the end of the line. Keller put a hand on his shoulder. "Let's go, boy."

"Okay," Cobb mumbled. He rolled over, his face sullen.

Back in his private room, Sergeant Keller slipped into his fatigue jacket. He felt vaguely uneasy. Combat boots were thudding down the hall, the men groaned and shouted. It's some type of shakedown, Keller thought. But what kind? There wasn't any liquor in the barracks, the Old Man knew that. They wouldn't pull a medical check at this hour of the night. Maybe it had something to do with the gasoline that was being stolen from the motor pool. But what could they prove by routing out the men at three in the A.M.?

Zippering his jacket, Sergeant Keller walked quickly down the corridor and out into the frigid air. He frowned, looking at the company street. The entire battalion was lined up, shuffling nervously, irritably in the freezing darkness. The blue arc lights were lit in the front of the barracks, their glow weak and wavering on the pounded snow.

Keller put on his gloves and took his place at the head of Headquarters Company. "Sarge," someone called, "what's happening?"

"I know as much as you do," Keller said.

"Some guy said there's Criminal Investigation men in battalion headquarters. Are there?"

"Don't know," Keller said. "Quiet in the ranks."

Keller stood naturally at ease, doubling his hands behind him, working them for warmth. He saw a small group of men approaching from battalion headquarters, their stride briskly professional in the snowy roadway.

"That's them," someone said. "CID in plainclothes."

"Knock it off!" Keller said.

The group came to a halt in front of headquarters barracks. There were four strange men in olive overcoats with Lieutenant Bracken, the battalion O.D. They stood silently for a few moments, surveying the ranks. Then one of them, a tall man, nodded to the lieutenant.

"This will be short and quick!" the lieutenant shouted. "Just follow instructions! If not we'll be here all night!"

The battalion had hushed. The street was silent except for the ragged moan of wind from the hills. Keller studied the faces of the four men in plainclothes. They were CID all right. He had seen their kind before, in Mannheim on a larceny investigation. But why were they here?

"Everyone will hold out their hands palms-up!" Lieutenant Bracken shouted. "Palms-up! If you're wearing gloves, get them off! Come on! I want to see those hands!"

Keller stripped off his gloves and extended his arms. The CID men had split up, one man to each company. The one for Headquarters came over to Keller. He turned the stabbing beam of a large flashlight on the sergeant's palms. Try as he could to control them, his thin hands trembled. "Turn 'em over," the man said. Keller obeyed. The flashlight washed them again. Then the man turned and marched over to the first rank.

Time dragged in the company street. Keller was too nervous to check his watch. The silence was broken only by the thin shuffle of feet on ice, a few soft questions and tense answers. Sometimes the flashlights bobbed, touching the panes of second-floor windows.

Finally, the group of four men went back to Lieutenant Bracken.

"All right," Bracken shouted. "Company sergeants will dismiss their men!"

Keller turned, pivoting, and gave the order. The men stirred and sluggishly began to file back to the barracks.

The C.Q. was waiting for Keller in his room. "I got the whole story," he said proudly.

Keller sank down wearily on his bed. "What?"

"Somebody killed a German taxi driver, an old guy. Rolled him and took all his money. Right outside the gate, too!"

"When?"

"A little before one o'clock. The CID were called in by the M.P.s. They narrowed it down to someone in this battalion."

Keller nodded and began pulling off his boots. "Figures. That's an old trick of theirs, checkin' the hands. They figure the guy might've got scratched or something."

"Well, like I said, it was an old guy. Couldn't have been much of a fight."

Keller felt the muscles tighten suddenly around his heart. Fight. Cobb had been out of breath when he came in. And he had returned at one o'clock.

"What's wrong, Sarge?" the fat boy asked.

Keller dropped his boots with a clatter on the floor. "Nothing, son. You better get some sleep."

The sergeant undressed and lay wide-awake under his blankets. All he could think of was Cobb's face and the hoarse rasp of his labored breathing.

The following afternoon, Sergeant Keller left his section early and returned to the empty barracks to shower and shave. In the day room he checked his name again on the guard roster. There was no mistake – "Keller, Benj. SGT of the Guard." His eyes ran down the rest of the column to a name under "Privates of the Guard." Peter

Cobb.

Under the needling pressure of the shower, Keller tried to relax, but he couldn't. Shaving in the steamy mirror he nicked himself twice. He went to his locker and dressed slowly for guard mount. On his way to the arms room to secure his weapon, he passed Cobb walking toward the barracks. Their eyes met, held, and then both moved on. Keller's face felt hot in the icy air.

He handed the private his receipt for the carbine and waited while the boy hunted among the gun racks. "Here you are, Sarge."

Taking the weapon, Keller ran a cleaning rod through its bore, inspecting the small grains of dirt on the dry cotton patch. He rubbed linseed oil on the stock, polishing it with hard strokes. Footsteps sounded on the stairs. A moment later Cobb, dressed for guard mount, came into the room. Keller didn't look at him, kept his eyes fixed on the gleaming stock of the gun. He heard movements that told him the private had brought Cobb his weapon.

Steeling himself, Keller looked up at Cobb. The man was swabbing his bore with a cleaning rod. Keller tried to keep his face relaxed. There was nothing to be afraid of, the gun was empty. But tonight there would be a steel clip in Cobb's carbine – with three bullets resting on the coiled spring to be ejected, if desired, into the weapon's chamber. And Cobb would be carrying that weapon for several hours while he walked his post.

Keller slung his rifle and ducked through the door. While descending the stairs to the ground level, he thought he heard Cobb laugh.

Guard mount lasted only a few minutes. Keller had prepared the privates of the guard for inspection, his eyes not once meeting Cobb's. Captain Campbell was the Officer of the Day. He was a huge, solid man, well over six feet tall, with a tired, remote face. During the ceremony he asked few questions of the men, grunted a great deal, and seemed satisfied to get out of the cold when it was over. Keller didn't like him, never had. He was a lazy officer and most people knew it.

Keller found out exactly how lazy Campbell was a few hours

later. The Captain called him into the O.D.'s private quarters, where he was already stretched out on a cot. "Keller," Campbell drawled, "I want you to make a special check on the late relief at the motor pool. Okay?"

Keller nodded stolidly, thinking: the so-and-so. It's his duty to go out there and do the checking. I'll never get any sleep.

"Gasoline's being stolen," Campbell continued. "Whoever's getting it has been selling the stuff to the Germans. Maybe you'll catch somebody tonight. Anyway, alert the guard and keep tabs."

Keller nodded.

"That's all, Sergeant. And get one of the privates to go down to the snack bar and bring me a black and white milkshake."

Keller went quietly back to battalion headquarters. The long building was empty now, most of the men had gone to the barrack or cleared post. Keller turned the lights on against the gray, hazy dusk that descended like snow from the Bavarian hills. He sat down behind the desk in the big, overheated room and looked at the field telephone. He twisted nervously in the chair, drummed his cold fingers on the blotter. Finally, he picked up the receiver and rang the guardroom. A corporal answered.

"Everything – all right over there?" Keller asked. He found it difficult to control his voice.

"All shaped up, Sarge."

"Tell me – when does Private Cobb go on relief?"

"Cobb? He's on last. Eleven o'clock. Walkin' the motor pool."

The motor pool. God, he'd have to check him. Cobb all alone down there with a loaded carbine.

"Sarge? You there?"

"Yes."

"You wanna be relieved for chow? I just ate, I'll cover for you."

"I – don't feel particularly hungry. Thanks anyway." Keller hung up. He rubbed his face and looked through the window. A guard, the first relief, was walking by outside, his carbine on his shoulder.

It would be the perfect chance for Cobb, Keller thought, feeling sick. He must have guessed that I know. All he has to do is see me coming. Then he could shoot me and claim I didn't identify myself. An accident. They'd investigate and hush it up, probably transfer him to another battalion.

Keller sat stupefied, the fear riding him. God, I'm acting silly! he thought. How do I really know who killed that taxi driver? So Cobb was out of breath, so he had a guilty look on his face. Maybe he was in a fight in town. I don't have any proof that he did the killing.

And then another part of his mind whispered: You saw his eyes, you saw his face last night. He did it. Don't try to fool yourself. He did it. And he knows you know. And you've got to go down to that dark motor pool tonight and check him out.

Keller slammed his fist down on the desk. The dusk outside was deepening into darkness. A Jeep rumbled by.

Keller closed his eyes, tried to shut out the insinuating voice in his mind. You can be killed tonight, it said. You can be shot down when you go to the motor pool. And there's no way you can escape it.

"I'm crazy!" he said aloud, and then, embarrassed, looked about to see if any of the guards had come in and heard him. But no one was there.

The telephone rang.

Keller jumped involuntarily, bumping his ankle on the chair. He bit his lip to ease the quick pain, then answered the phone.

"Captain Campbell, Sergeant," the voice drawled in his ear. "I'm turning in now, don't feel so well. Remember to check the late relief in the pool."

This is your chance, that inner voice said. Tell him everything, all your suspicions about Cobb. He'll believe you; he'll investigate.

I'll tell him, Keller thought. I'll tell him! But then he hesitated, and he knew he wouldn't. Eleven years of taking orders, obeying them, never questioning, never alienating, froze his voice. "Yes, sir, I'll check," he choked out.

"Good night."

Keller hung, up his hand shaking. It's only a ridiculous fear, he told himself. Cobb didn't kill anybody; he won't be waiting for me. I've blown this thing out of proportion. It's a trick of the mind. I'm acting like a raw recruit!

He got up and went over to the window. At the far end of the street, an arc light glinted on a helmet liner. The first relief, relieved, was returning to the guardroom. Keller pressed his face to the cold glass, watching him trudge through the soft-shining banks of snow. In two hours Cobb would be walking the motor pool.

Keller washed his face in the officers' sink. His head was blazing, almost as if he had a fever. He roamed about the desks and then sat down again, thinking hard. Not one mistake in eleven years. Caution combined with common sense, that had always been his secret. Old Play-It-Safe. He had survived two wars with that philosophy. And now, tonight, all of it wiped away. Just because that lazy do-nothing Campbell had given him an order, he had to put himself in a position where he might be killed. He lowered his head on his arms, using the desktop as a support. Well, he wouldn't go down to the pool. The hell with Campbell. If he checked and found that he hadn't obeyed the order, well, they would have to court martial him. His life was more important than that. Maybe Cobb wasn't involved at all; maybe it was just his imagination. But it wasn't worth taking the chance.

At peace now, satisfied with his decision, Sergeant Keller closed his eyes. He slept.

The telephone rang at eleven o'clock. Keller woke with a start, dazed and guilty. My God! he thought. How long have I slept?

He picked up the phone and answered.

"Captain Campbell, Sergeant. I just got a call from the M.P. Station. They picked up the man who killed that taxi driver. He's in our battalion, Charlie Company. They just got a full confession from him. Found the money he stole."

Keller was still sleepy, but the Captain's words revived him. "What's – what's his name, sir?"

"Gruber, Huber, something like that. You know the man?"

"No, sir, I don't."

"Well, they have him in custody and they're bringing him back here. We'll have to put him under guard until tomorrow morning. Take care of it, will you?"

Keller smiled. "Yes, sir!" And then he remembered. "But I have to check out the motor pool guard. It's eleven, sir."

"Well – they should be here any minute with the prisoner. No,

I guess it's all right. Check down there and then get right back."

"Yes, sir."

Campbell hung up.

Sergeant Keller felt almost joyful with relief. I really went off the deep end there for a while, he told himself. Funny what the mind can do, the way it can make something out of nothing. Buttoning on his heavy parka, he was suddenly glad that he hadn't mentioned anything to Cobb. He hated making apologies.

The battalion motor pool was only two blocks from battalion headquarters, a long, cold field filled with heavy equipment. Sergeant Keller ducked under the draw-gate and headed for the line of low sheds, the guard's area. He walked quickly, his hands thrust deep down in the parka's pockets.

A truck was drawn up behind the first shed. A few dark figures were rolling gasoline drums out of the shadowed building.

"Hey!" Keller called. "What's going on there?"

One of the figures moved away from the shed and Keller saw that it was Cobb. The soldier bent over one of the drums and picked up a carbine. "Halt!" he yelled.

"Halt, hell!" Keller shouted. The gasoline. They were stealing the gasoline. And Cobb was helping them. He began to run toward the truck.

The night exploded. Keller saw the bright flash and felt the burning pain almost simultaneously. He staggered and fell in the snow.

Dimly, distantly, he heard the truck start and pull away. Footsteps crunched on ice, drawing closer. It was an effort, but Sergeant Keller opened his eyes and saw Cobb's face, the carbine smoking in his hand.

"You should've stayed in bed, Sarge," Cobb said mockingly. "Now look what I've done. I've gone and had me an accident."

But Sergeant Keller didn't hear him.

ROBBERY, ROBBERY, ROBBERY

Charles Henderson stood behind the teller's window, counting hundred-dollar bills into a neat pile. He was a serious young man in his late twenties, with a crisp crew cut and an innocent, collegiate face. It was growing hot in the small enclosure, and he felt a drop of sweat on his temple.

"Your window open?" a voice said.

Henderson glanced up at a tall, powerful man who had come over to his counter. "Yes, sir," he said.

The man watched him for a moment. Something seemed to be troubling him. His face, to Henderson, was vaguely familiar.

"Can I help you?"

"I think so." The man slid a cotton bag under the bars of the window. He lifted the bag slightly and Henderson suddenly noticed that there was a .38 pistol beneath it, pointing at his stomach. "Fill it up," the man said softly. "Everything you've got."

Henderson stared at the gun, his throat tightening. "Listen, you –"

"Make it quick," the man said. "No talk."

Henderson fumbled at the drawstring of the bag. He turned his head, scanning the other two tellers working a few feet away. Mr. Powers, the manager, was sitting in his office.

"Did you hear me?"

Henderson nodded and began dumping the money into the bag. His eyes dropped below the polished ledge of the window to the brass-colored alarm button. Forget it, he told himself. What will playing the hero get me? My name in the papers? He stuffed the rest of the money into the bag and began drawing the string.

"Hold on," said the man. "You're not finished. Let's have that money on the table behind you."

Henderson nodded slowly, and re-opened the bag. He swept the currency inside, marveling at the incongruity of his thoughts.

It's too hot in here. Why doesn't Powers put in air-conditioning? Thursday morning. Have to get a haircut this afternoon.

He handed the man the bag, and again had the feeling that he had seen him before. He studied the narrow, bright eyes, the pocked skin, the white scar tissue along the sallow jaw.

The man pulled the bag's string tight with his teeth. Two missing in the lower jaw, Henderson thought. Then he watched as the man walked quickly away from the counter, moved across the bank, and spun through the revolving doors. The man was running when he reached the pavement.

The whole thing had taken less than a minute. Henderson looked around the small bank. The two tellers were calmly checking file cards; Powers was patting the shoulder of an old lady in his private office. Henderson smiled slightly, amused by his own detachment, and pressed the alarm button.

Powers handed him a paper cup of ice water. The bank was closed; the venetian blinds had been lowered against the white noon light. A plainclothesman was sprinkling powder over the ledge of the teller's window.

"How do you feel, Henderson?" Powers asked him.

Henderson smiled. "All right." He liked the gray, worried look on Powers' face. Maybe this afternoon would be a perfect time to ask for that raise.

"Henderson?" A big, awkward-moving man had entered the office. "Lieutenant Pissano, Robbery," he said with authority. "You okay?"

Henderson decided he would feign the weak, frightened bank teller. Pissano seemed to want that, anyway. "I'm pretty shaky, Lieutenant. That was a terrible experience."

"Yeah, I guess it was," Pissano said sympathetically. "What'd he look like?"

Henderson watched him open a neat leather notebook. Amused, he debated whether he should give a wrong description, just for the hell of it. He decided not to; they might eventually catch the man. "He was tall," Henderson said finally. "Average-looking. That's really about all I can give you."

"Suppose you think hard," Pissano said.

Henderson rebelled against the man's tone. He didn't need the superior attitude. "Sorry, Lieutenant. My mind's a blank."

Powers was still nervous. "Try to think, Henderson."

"What was he wearing?" Pissano asked.

"I really don't remember. I think he had a scar on his face, though."

Pissano jotted it down. "Where was this scar?"

"On his jaw."

Another notation. "How'd he talk? Regional accent?"

"I don't know. Like you and me."

Pissano checked his notebook. "Okay. Let me have your address and phone number. We might have a few pictures we'll want you to look at."

Henderson gave him the information. "I've got a splitting headache, Lieutenant," he added. "Are you finished with me?"

Pissano nodded. He looked at Powers and went over to the fingerprint man.

"You'd better take the rest of the day off," Powers said. "We're going to close up anyway."

Henderson nodded. He stood up and pretended a feeling of faintness.

"Hey, you'd better take it easy," Powers said.

"I'll be all right. See you tomorrow morning at nine sharp."

"Well, if you're not feeling well tomorrow, perhaps..."

"No, that's okay." He turned to Powers. Now was as good a time as any. "Listen, Mr. Powers, I was wanting to talk to you. I've been here eight months now..."

It was warm in his apartment and he turned on the fan. In the kitchen he stripped off his jacket and poured himself a glass of cold milk. He was feeling reasonably good. Powers had come through with a five dollar raise; no protest whatsoever.

He went into the bedroom, where it was cooler, and stretched out on the bed. He had the robbery to thank. Powers had lowered his defenses because of it and had been wide open for the raise. Maybe he should have asked for ten bucks.

While lying on the bed, his conscious mind at rest, he suddenly remembered where he had seen the holdup man. Startled and pleased, he swung his legs over the edge of the bed and sat there for a moment, thinking.

There had been a diner across town, where he had eaten regularly the previous year. And behind the counter had been a tall, powerful man with pockmarked skin and scar tissue.

Henderson prodded his memory. The face of the diner cook merged with the face of the man in the bank. They were the same.

He got to his feet and went back to the kitchen, turning off the fan. I wonder if he's still there? he thought. Then he saw his jacket thrown over the back of a chair. He picked it up and stroked the material aimlessly with his fingers. It was still bright out, no sign of rain. Why not check on the guy? He had a free afternoon with nothing else to do. And it might be interesting.

Abruptly, he put on his jacket and went to the door.

The Edgewood Diner was almost empty in mid-afternoon. The owner was listening to a disk jockey and the hired help were frying themselves hamburgers on the grill.

Henderson sat down at the counter and ordered a cup of coffee. "Where's the guy who works the stove?" he asked the owner.

"Wallace? Out sick today. He'll be back tomorrow."

Henderson dug a coin out of his pocket and put it on the counter. "I owe him some money. Thought he'd be in."

"Tomorrow," the man said. He took the coin.

"Anyplace I can reach him?"

An elderly Negro turned from the grill. "Lives over on Walnut, mister. Three-sixteen."

"He got a phone over there, do you know?"

"Pay phone in the hall. Turner 6-6132."

"Henderson smiled. "You're well informed."

The Negro grinned back. "Owes me money, man. He oughta stop playin' cards. He's just plain stupid."

Henderson finished his coffee and left.

There was a drugstore across the street from Wallace's building. Henderson dialed the Turner number and counted the rings. The sixth was cut short. "Hello?"

"Wallace?"

There was a short pause. "Who's this?"

"A friend."

"You've got the wrong number, friend."

"I don't think so. Let's talk about the money, Wallace." There was no answer. "You still there?"

"Who is this?"

Henderson paused. It sounded like the same voice, but he couldn't be sure. "You don't know me. But I know you, Wallace. I even know where you were this morning."

"What are you talkin' about?"

"Suppose you meet me at —" Henderson checked his watch. "Four o'clock. That's five minutes from now. At the corner of Walnut and Third."

"Now look —"

"All I have to do is drop another dime in this phone and call the police."

There was a long pause. "Okay," Wallace said. "Four o'clock. Walnut and Third." He hung up.

Henderson replaced the receiver and left the booth. At the front of the drugstore was a large glass window that overlooked the street and the adjacent boarding houses. He bought a pack of cigarettes and stationed himself by the window, keeping his eye on the door of number 316. A few minutes later a man came out and walked down the steps to the street. Henderson smiled, recognizing the powerful frame and the sallow face. He waited until the man had turned the corner and then he left the drugstore.

He checked the number on the hall pay phone and then tried the door at the end of the dark corridor. It was locked. He stood for a brief moment with his hand on the knob, watching where the rickety staircase melted in shadows. Wallace would probably be gone, at the most, ten minutes.

Henderson hurled his body at the door. Again. The third time the flimsy lock gave and he stumbled, almost falling, into the room. It was a cramped cubicle, papered in hideous purple, and a smeared window overlooked a tangle of alleys and backyards. Henderson went over to the bed and ripped off the covers, tossed the mattress on the floor. He opened the drawers of a cheap pine bureau, but most of them were empty. There was nothing in the closet except some hangers and a small suitcase. The suitcase, when he opened it, contained nothing but a pair of socks.

He came back to the center of the room and scanned the walls for some area of concealment. It was dim in the room and he found himself wishing for more light. Then he looked up. A glass lighting fixture hung on two chains from the ceiling.

Smiling, Henderson climbed on the bed and swung at the light bowl. His fingertips brushed its bottom. He jumped and swung again, this time catching it with the side of his hand. The bowl bounced and tilted, and then a cotton bag slid out and fell to the floor. Henderson sprang from the bed and opened the drawstring of the bag. It was filled with the bank money.

Henderson checked his watch (five more minutes) and looked around. He'd need something to put the bag in; he couldn't carry it around like it was. Then he remembered the suitcase in the closet. He took it out, stuffed in the bag, and closed the clasps. A few minutes later he was descending the staircase, swinging the suitcase and whistling softly.

His nerves, exhilarated by the afternoon's experience, needed calming. After walking the streets for a while, he went into a bar and took a booth in the back, wedging the suitcase tightly between his legs. He ordered a drink and sat nursing it, thinking back over the past hour. It had been so easy, so incredibly easy. He didn't remember at what point he had decided to take the money, but it didn't matter. It was all over now. The only moment of danger had been in the room with the possibility of Wallace returning early, but that was in the past.

Henderson left the bar after a second drink and took a bus home, watching the warm dusk come down, the growing neon. He would have to hide the money for a while – eight months, perhaps a year. The precaution would be worth it. Then it would be his to spend on the car, the trip to Europe, the women. He smiled at the beautiful irony of the situation. Wallace was power-less; he could never go to the police and report the robbery. The money had been twice stolen.

He got off the bus a few blocks before his stop and walked slow-ly, enjoying the twilight. When he reached his street, a black car pulled up to the curb. "Henderson?"

He stopped abruptly, his hand tightening on the suitcase. The driver was a stout, middle-aged man, someone he had never seen before. But Pissano was sitting beside him, looking through the lowered window. "We've just been at your apartment," he said. His eyes dropped to the suitcase. "You planning on going on a trip or something, Henderson? Huh?"

"No, Lieutenant. I was walking home." He lifted the suitcase. "I just have some things in here that I picked up in town."

"Mind coming down to the station with us? It won't take more than an hour."

"The station? What for?"

"Routine stuff. Hop in."

Henderson shifted uneasily on the curb. "Well, could I drop off this suitcase? No sense in carting it along."

"Take it with you. We're in a hurry."

Henderson opened the rear door and climbed in. He put the suitcase on the floor and rested his feet on top of it.

The stout man started the motor and pulled away from the curb. Pissano turned around and studied Henderson. "How do you feel?"

"Much better, thanks." He leaned forward. "What do you want to do down at the station?"

"Routine," Pissano said. "We think maybe we can wrap this thing up tonight."

He turned back and was silent for the rest of the ride.

Henderson sat in what seemed to be a small, dim auditorium. There was a long platform in the front, containing a speaker's stand and a microphone. The area was garishly lit by a string of powerful lights recessed in the ceiling. Pissano moved past Henderson and sat down next to him. "You gonna move that suitcase?" he said. "It's sorta blocking the aisle."

Henderson nodded. He picked it up and set it on the empty seat next to him. "What's going to happen?" he said.

"There'll be a half-dozen men coming out on that platform. I want you to take a good look at them. Tell me if anyone seems familiar."

A uniformed policeman came from a doorway and stood at the speaker's stand. He said into the microphone: "All right, let's move it, boys. You won't melt under the lights. Let's go."

Henderson watched six men shamble out and stand lounging against the rear wall. This should be rather amusing, he thought. They must have combed Skid Row for these bums. Feeling relaxed for the first time since Pissano picked him up, he took out a cigarette and lit a match. And then his head jerked up. Across six feet of empty chairs in the darkened room his eyes met those of Wallace, the last man on the platform.

"What's wrong?" Pissano said eagerly. "You recognize someone?"

"No," Henderson said. It was difficult keeping his voice normal. The match, raised to his lips, burned brightly, illuminating his face. He started to shake it out with a numb finger, but not before Wallace lowered his gaze. Panic-stricken, Henderson watched the man stare at the suitcase on the seat beside him. He saw recognition break over Wallace's face, and then anger. He dropped the match, still flaming.

Pissano was looking at him. "You sure, Henderson?"

"Yes."

The policeman on the platform was having each man step forward and remove his hat if he wore one. He asked several of them questions and received abrupt, surly answers. Eventually Wallace stepped up, still staring through the lights at Henderson.

"Your name?" the policeman asked.

"Wallace."

"Your full name, Wallace."

"Art Wallace." He brought a hand up to shade his eyes.

"Take your hand away from your face!"

Wallace dropped it. His mouth twisted in a quiet, growing anger.

"Nothing, huh?" Pissano asked.

Henderson lowered his head. "No."

Pissano stood up. The six men were filing out. "Well," he said, "maybe the next time." He shook his head. "I really thought one of these babies was our boy. They were all involved in bank jobs in the past. Picked 'em up this afternoon. It only goes to show you."

The room was empty now except for the two of them and the policeman on the platform. "Are you holding those men?" Henderson asked.

"No, they'll be released in a few minutes. Nothing to hold them on."

Henderson got to his feet, slowly. He groped toward the aisle. "Can – I go now, Lieutenant?"

"Sure. We'll probably have a new batch for you tomorrow. Pick you up at the bank."

Henderson lifted the suitcase. It felt heavier, almost a burden.

"Get some rest," Pissano said. "You don't look too good."

He nodded. "Good night, Lieutenant."

"'Night. Sorry to bring you down here on a wild goose chase. But you never know."

Henderson moved to the door. "Could – you give me a lift back?"

"Afraid not. I think the cars are tied up. And I'll be here for a couple more hours. Take a cab. We'll reimburse you tomorrow. I wouldn't wander around the neighborhood; it's a pretty bad one, especially at night."

Henderson stepped through the door. He stood in a small, brick alleyway. He hurried along it and emerged on the pavement beside the police station. A block away a few cars moved sluggishly on a dim thoroughfare. He walked quickly toward it.

Have to get away from here, he thought, looking over his shoulder. Wallace spotted me and recognized his damn suitcase. Everything's in his favor now. I didn't identify him. He could kill me and take back the money; the police would never suspect him again. I didn't point him out.

He reached the street and stopped, looking in both directions. There were no cabs or buses. The neighborhood was deserted; it was a good several miles from the main arteries of the city. And Wallace, having been released, was probably looking for him.

Henderson turned, hurried off, the suitcase dragging at his ankles. He headed down a lane of shabby, closed buildings. Something moved at the end of the block. A man's figure.

Henderson swung around and started in the opposite direction. He would go back to the police station; he had been a fool to leave in the first place. They had phones. He could call a cab from there. Henderson looked around. Was the man a block or two behind him? To his right? He could hear footsteps approaching.

He cut into a side street, stumbled into a trashcan, and sent it clanging across the curb. Buildings again, high and black, on either side. The sky was dark, starless.

Henderson started running. There seemed to be no end to the street. He heard, close behind him, the accelerated tap of feet, echoing the sound of his own. He tried to go faster, but he suddenly felt dead tired. Finally he stopped, pressing himself against the brick wall of a building.

A shadow appeared, lengthening on the pavement, touching the bottom of the wall. Henderson turned his face to the bricks, still trying to draw concealment from them. The footsteps came up behind him and stopped. Henderson dropped the suitcase. "Look, Wallace –" he said. He turned around.

Lieutenant Pissano finished the water in a paper cup, crushed it, and dropped it in the wastepaper basket. He went over to the desk and looked down at the short, chunky boy who sat in the shaft of light from the overhead lamp.

"Okay, punk," he said, "let's get it straight. You followed him, you tried to take his wallet, he put up a struggle, and when he put up a struggle you stabbed him."

The boy looked up. His face was dirty. "He didn't fight me. He just started laughin' as soon as he saw who I was. Laughin' and laughin'. I told him to keep quiet. I told him."

"But he didn't so you stabbed him?"

The boy's face dropped forward on his hands. Pissano walked to a table. Displayed on it was a suitcase, a wallet, several coins, a handkerchief, and a package of cigarettes. Pissano opened the wallet. "Three bucks. You killed him for three bucks."

"I didn't mean it."

"Shut up!" Pissano felt sick to his stomach. If he hadn't brought Henderson to the station, if he had given him transportation home…He dropped the wallet on the table. "Take him downstairs," he told a uniformed policeman who stood near the door. "And file these things until Henderson's kin pick them up."

The policeman crossed to the boy. "On your feet, son."

Aimlessly, Pissano dropped the coins through his fingers. He picked up the handkerchief and looked at it, shaking his head. Then he began to unfasten the clasps of the suitcase to open it.

"I didn't mean it," said the boy, starting for the door. "He must've been crazy, laughin' like that. He thought I was someone else, too. Kept callin' me Wallace."

Lieutenant Pissano was silent. He stood looking into the open suitcase for a moment. Then he turned to the boy, his face thoughtful. "Wallace…?" he said with growing comprehension.

THE HUNDRED-DOLLAR BIRD'S NEST

Doctor Mowbray sat on the cool wooden porch of Mrs. Parsons' boarding house, enjoying the view of the garden. He was a big, raw-boned man, ponderously meditative, with sparse, dirty gray hair. His seersucker jacket was open over his swelling paunch.

He leaned back in the wicker chair and placed a black cigar in his mouth, lighting it with a paper match. Inhaling the smoke, he surveyed the small garden through narrowed eyes. Spring had come; he could feel its budding in his old bones. There were bees droning in the green bushes, birds circling, searching overhead. He watched a robin building a nest in the elm tree across the yard.

Doctor Mowbray reflected on the warm scene with a growing sense of unfulfillment. He was sixty-eight last December – a lost old man with only six hundred dollars in the bank. His marriage had been childless; his wife was dead. He coughed on the cigar smoke, wiped his smarting eyes. If only he had planned, managed to save his money. Where had it all gone? On Marjorie's parties, on mellow bourbon, on the moist noses of trotting horses on the summer racetracks. And now with his heart trouble, a practice was out of the question.

Doctor Mowbray closed his eyes and the daydreams descended. He could picture himself taking a Caribbean cruise, or sunning himself on the lush shores of the Riviera. That was the way to die. Not sitting on the porch of a rotting boarding house, smoking a dime cigar, while the world, the real world, spun brightly out of reach.

The door opened and a pretty young girl walked past his chair. "Good morning, Doctor," she said, smiling.

"Morning, Doris."

He watched her full, fresh figure walk down the wooden steps and move through the garden. God, she's lucky, he thought. Young and pretty on the threshold of summer. She would be swimming and out with her friends in open convertibles. If only he had a car. Even an old one would do. He would take a long trip north, to the fir country, maybe Quebec.

Doctor Mowbray tossed his bitter cigar over the porch railing and looked up as the door opened again. Mr. Shantz stepped out, a thin, bald old man wearing a wrinkled woolen suit. He shuffled past Mowbray, his head lowered, and clumped awkwardly down the stairs.

"Morning, Mr. Shantz," the doctor said.

Shantz didn't answer. He moved quickly through the garden and out the white-picket gate.

Queer old duck, Mowbray thought. Worn that same suit every day for the past two years. Mrs. Parsons had a devil of a time getting him to pay his board. I guess I'm not so bad off after all. What does Shantz have? No friends, no money, just a sour disposition.

He stood up and stretched. It was eleven o'clock and the porch was growing warm. "Want some lemonade, Doctor?" Mrs. Parson called from the window.

"No thanks, ma'am," the doctor said. He went down into the garden and felt the full heat of the sun on his face. The bees droned louder, the whole yard seemed to murmur. Doctor Mowbray looked up. The sky was filled with sun and birds. He watched a robin suddenly dart out from a window ledge on the top floor of the boarding house. It had a piece of paper in its beak.

Mowbray smiled. Spring, he thought. Time to build and save. The robin settled, chirping, on the new nest in the elm tree. The Doctor walked over. Smart creatures, the birds, he thought. They search all over for straw and paper, they find what they can and they build their nests. Security. Much smarter than humans sometimes.

He stood by the tree and watched the robin hopping about in the twigs, the piece of paper in its beak. The paper curled in a slight breeze. My God! Mowbray thought. He moved closer and peered up at the busy bird. He was right. It had what looked like a dollar-bill in its mouth.

Carefully, he leaned against the trunk, raised his hand over his head. He snatched at the bill. The bird flew off in a blur of feathers, but Mowbray had the money. He looked at it in the sharp light and his tired heart tripped faster. He had been wrong. It wasn't a dollar; it was a hundred-dollar bill. Benjamin Franklin's picture looked up at him from the creased paper.

Doctor Mowbray was stunned for an instant. He studied the blank windows of the boarding house. Mrs. Parsons was probably in the kitchen, no one was watching him. He crumpled the bill and slipped it in his coat pocket. Amazing, he thought. Where had the bird come across it?

His eyes lifted, traveled up the weathered, gabled façade of the old house. Up and up until he was staring at the tall window on the last floor where the robin had alighted. That was Shantz's room, the reconverted attic. But Shantz was dirt-poor, couldn't even pay his board most months. What was he doing with a hundred-dollar bill?

Doctor Mowbray moved back to the porch, his hand working the smooth paper in his pocket. He stood under the maple rafters, musing over his discovery. The bird had flown into Shantz's room, found the bill and carried it to its nest. Was there more of the same up there?

In the kitchen, Mrs. Parsons was shelling peas. She glanced up as Doctor Mowbray came in. "Any of that lemonade left?" he asked her.

"Whole pitcherful. Help yourself, Doc."

He opened the cupboard and reached in for a glass. He noted the keys hanging on a screw in the back wall of the cabinet. He closed the door and slowly poured a glass of lemonade from the pitcher.

"Getting hot already," Mrs. Parsons said.

"Yep. Spring doesn't last long anymore."

"Goin' away this summer, Doc?"

"Maybe."

The telephone rang in the dining room. Mrs. Parsons wiped her hands and hurried off to answer it.

Doctor Mowbray set the glass in the sink and opened the cupboard door. He took the keys from the screw and pocketed them.

They slid down next to the folded bill. Then he closed the door and finished his glass of lemonade.

It was a long, hard climb to the fourth floor. He was winded when he reached it, sweat running down his pink forehead. He stopped, panting, on the landing, and steadied himself on the banister. Old Shantz's door was closed, locked tight.

He inserted the master key in the lock and twisted it gently. There was a dull click and he opened the door. It smelled old and musty in the bright, attic room. Place needed a good spring cleaning, Mowbray thought.

He closed the door and looked around. There was nothing under the bed except a gray mat of cobwebs. Use your head, the doctor cautioned himself. If the bird got it, it must be somewhere fairly out in the open. There wasn't any other furniture in the room except for a rocking chair and a big, solid bureau. He went to the bureau and poked around its top. Just a battered alarm clock and a few old souvenirs. And the drawers were closed – the robin couldn't have opened them.

He noticed then that the bureau stood a good few inches from the wall. He moved around it and looked down. Sure enough! There was a box wedged tightly between the wall and the bureau. He dug his hand down deep and came up with a fistful of wadded bills. Some were rolled in green cones, others were loose, some were folded into crazy, intricate patterns. Anchoring the money, lying on top of it, was an ancient pistol. He replaced the bills and backed away.

That filthy old miser, he thought angrily. There must be thousands in that box. Tries to cheat Mrs. Parsons out of her money and has a fortune hidden behind his bureau! And what's he do with it? Doesn't spend a penny; wears that same old suit every day of his life.

Doctor Mowbray wiped the sweat from his face and leaned over the sill of the wide, open window. The fresh air felt warm, but good. Birds sang in the high elm. His eyes ranged out past the picket fence, across the emerald fields to where a stooped figure was hurrying down the road. Shantz!

Doctor Mowbray clattered toward the door. He locked it and

stumbled down the staircase.

A few minutes later he was back in the wicker chair on the porch. He lit a cigar with a faintly trembling hand. "Morning, Mr. Shantz," he said.

"Morning." Shantz walked quickly up the stairs and shot him a glance.

"Getting rather hot out," the doctor said.

Shantz nodded and entered the house.

Mowbray let out his breath and shook his gray head. He was irritated with himself; he should have taken the money while he had the chance and hidden it in his room. But Shantz's return had rattled him.

The money was still there, of course. He could take it away at any time. But if he did? Mowbray speculated for a moment, tapping his fingers on the sunny arm of the chair. If he robbed Shantz, the old man would scream to the police. There would be a search, questions. The members of the household would be immediate suspects. They would be watched, their actions traced. And if old Doctor Mowbray suddenly decided to take a trip, why, where did he get the money? Questions and more questions. No, robbery was not the way.

Mowbray left the chair and went into the kitchen to return Mrs. Parsons' keys. He was sure there was another solution.

It was early evening when Doctor Mowbray returned from his small dinner at the country roadhouse. Shantz was sitting in the stuffy living room reading Mrs. Parsons' morning paper. Mowbray sat down on the sofa and picked up a magazine. He flipped through the pages, then settled back, pretending to read. He had the strange, unfounded feeling that the other man was watching him over the rim of the paper. Finally, he rose and went silently upstairs to his room.

He paced about for almost an hour, his mind veering off in violent directions. Shantz was an old man, a septuagenarian. Mowbray had treated him last winter, when he complained about pains around his heart.

Mowbray took his dusty medical bag out of the closet. He still

had a small bottle of cardiac medicine, the special digitalis prepa-
rations he used on himself. An overdose would be fatal for a weak
heart.

He placed the bottle on his table and opened the window. He
felt the cool, brisk breeze on his dry skin. It would involve a dangerous chance, but the reward was worth it. He would have to
make Shantz take the medicine that night. The next morning,
probably around noon, Mrs. Parsons would discover the body.
And who would be the first person she would call? Old Doctor
Mowbray, of course. It was perfect. He would declare death of old
age, and sign the certificate. Even if they investigated, they would
merely find that Shantz had taken an overdose of medicine. Since
there would be no apparent motive involved, he would go unsus-
pected. No one, after all, knew about the money.

It had grown dark in the garden and moths banged against
the screens. Doctor Mowbray watched them for a moment, then
removed a syringe from his medical bag. He plunged the needle
in the bottle and withdrew a few centimeters of the liquid. He
emptied the rest of the bottle into the sink, flushed it out with hot
tap water, and scratched the label off. He placed the syringe and a
small absorbent rag in the drawer of the table.

On the way downstairs he passed Shantz going up for the
night.

"Night," Doctor Mowbray said. Shantz didn't answer. He
clumped heavily up the stairs, asthmatic breath wheezing in
his gnarled throat. That's right, Mowbray thought. Climb those
stairs, keep a strain on that heart.

"Doc?" Mrs. Parsons asked. "You goin' over to the drugstore?
Get me a paper?"

"Not going over there particularly. But I'll pick you one up."

"Thanks, Doc. Lovely evenin'."

"Yes."

He walked slowly through the garden, smelling the rich night
earth, the early blossoms. His head was light, his step resilient.
He felt suddenly like a young man with the rush of spring in an
awakened body. He went through the picket gate and crossed the
road.

Doctor Anderson's house was on a quiet street of elderly maples. Mowbray visited him frequently for quiet evenings of shoptalk over rich bourbon. The young doctor's blond wife answered the door. "Charlie home?"

"I'm expecting him, Doc," she said. "Come on in."

They talked for a while in Anderson's office. Mowbray wandered to the glass-fronted cabinet and saw the bottle of chloroform sitting on one of the shelves. Now if she'd only leave the room.

"Say, Betty," he said. "How's the youngster?"

"Fine, Doc. I'm getting ready to feed him." She laughed. "Charlie says he's eating up the practice."

"Bring him in," said Mowbray. "I'd like to see him."

"All right."

She left the room.

Mowbray removed the bottle of chloroform and poured a portion into the empty cardiac bottle. It left a lingering odor in the air, and he opened a window. A moment later Betty came in with the baby. "Say hello to the doctor," she said.

Mowbray listened patiently while the child's more recent adventures were related, then he looked at his watch. "I guess I'd better be going, Betty. Tell Charlie I dropped by."

"Why don't you wait, Doc? He should be here in a few minutes."

"I'll see him tomorrow."

He left by the front door.

At the drugstore, he bought Mrs. Parsons her evening newspaper and walked slowly back to the boarding house, enjoying the cool air.

He left the paper in the parlor and went to his room. Leaning from his window, he could see the white rectangle of Shantz's window shining in the garden. It was growing late and the old house was still. Mowbray sat tensely on the windowsill, waiting, waiting. When was the old devil going to turn in? Didn't he know that a bad heart needed plenty of rest? The minutes ran by, the moon cleaving past the elm and brightening the garden. Far off, muffled by fields and homes, the town clock chimed midnight. A second later, Shantz's light went off.

Doctor Mowbray paced the room, careful not to set the boards creaking. Mrs. Parsons slept below, and he didn't want her to become suspicious of his late prowling. He would give the old man an hour, a full sixty minutes to fall asleep. That would be plenty of time for the stiff muscles to relax, the brain drain of blood, the pulse slow, grow dimmer.

The town clock chimed one, and Doctor Mowbray gathered his tools. The filled syringe, the cloth, and the bottle of chloroform. Fully asleep, Shantz would never feel the wet rag pressed carefully to his lips or the wasp-prick in his forearm. He would merely slip into a much deeper, darker sleep.

Doctor Mowbray went softly to the kitchen, opened the cupboard, and removed the keys. Then, measuring every footfall, he slowly ascended the stairs. The glass implements in his coat pocket tinkled once, and he quickly slid his hand in to separate them. Two more flights, that was all.

He made it and stopped breathing heavily in the dark. The last landing was bright with moonlight pouring in from the window, flooding Shantz's door.

He moved to the window and again stopped, listening. He removed the passkey from his trouser pocket. He stood there, one hand on the sill, motionless, staring at the closed door. He was about to move when a sound startled him. He jumped and peered out the window. Then he smiled.

There was a bird perched outside on the ledge. It looked like a robin. Doctor Mowbray watched it, wondering if it was the same one who had found the bill. He chuckled deep in his throat. Bird, he thought, if all goes well I'll buy you a cage of solid gold. You can come with me across the seas and travel the world.

Carefully, his hand perfectly steady, he inserted the key and turned it. The tumblers clicked and he slowly twisted the knob.

The young officer looked down at the sheet-covered body in the attic room. He opened his notebook and said, "Let's hear it again."

The thin, bald old man straightened his woolen suit. "I already told you, young man. I knew somebody was stealing my money."

"So you didn't go to sleep?"

"Nope. Just laid awake. Then I heard that key in the door. Nobody makes honest visits after midnight, so when he crept in I let him have it with my gun. I was in my rights."

The police officer nodded. The door was opening, and he hurriedly closed it against the crowd of tenants in nightdress who were gathered outside on the landing.

"That money's important to me," said Shantz. "Gonna use it someday. Gonna take a trip and see some things."

"One thing I don't understand," said the police officer. "How you know somebody was after your money?"

"I count it, young man. I count it every day." Shantz frowned. "And this afternoon there was a hundred-dollar bill missin'."

The police officer nodded as if in confirmation. He removed a bill from his pocket and showed it to the old man. "This must be it? We found it in his room."

"Yep. And I figured whoever took it would come back to get the rest." He laughed, a high cackle. "No question in my mind somebody took it. I mean, money don't just fly away, does it?"

ONE BAD WINTER DAY

Karl sat by the big, pot-bellied stove in his office, looking through the window. He was tired, and he could feel the weather in every joint. He found himself wishing that he could sleep all winter like a bear; that he could wake up in the spring when the trout were jumping and the woods were warm.

Well, he told himself, it was a matter of time. Retirement, a small monthly pension – just a matter of weeks. And then he would have all day for the sun, all day to read and fish and relax.

Al, the new deputy, rested his feet on the stove. "You ever seen my kid?" he asked. He handed Karl a small color photograph. "My wife took that," he said.

Karl looked at the round-faced infant. "Cute."

"We got another one on the way." He took the picture back. "This time we're going to get a movie camera and take pictures every month. Kind of a record, like."

Karl smiled. Sure loves his kid, he thought. Nice having children, having a good responsibility like that. He leaned back. It wouldn't be a bad afternoon, he decided. Maybe he'd send Al out for some coffee, if old man Wyco hadn't closed up due to the snow.

"Is it always quiet like this?" Al asked.

"When it snows it is. Nobody feels like acting up. Everybody just sits around looking at each other." He stretched back, yawning. "Maybe you want to go out and get some coffee?"

"That's okay with me." As Al got up, the telephone rang. "Wonder if that's my wife," he said.

Karl took it. It was a long-distance call from Denver. "Yes?"

"That you, Karl? Ed Gruen."

"Yeah. What's up, Ed?"

Al stopped by the doorway, then turned and came back slowly, tentatively.

"Bobby Lee broke out last night. He's headed your way."

"The hell you say. Alone?"

"Uh-huh. He wants to reach Larkspur or Kalen; he's got friends down there. He's wounded. We winged him in the hip."

Karl leaned forward in his chair. He had a funny feeling in his stomach. "What kind of a car's he got?"

"'Forty-eight Dodge sedan, all gray. He stole it. Look, you got any help down there?"

Karl looked at the white empty streets. "It's snowing," he said.

"I know. That's what's holding up the State Police. We'll try to have somebody up there by tonight." The hard voice paused. "Lee's got a Colt .45 job."

"Who is it?" Al asked.

"Okay, Ed," Karl said. "I'll see what I can do. Thanks for calling." The phone clicked dead.

Al leaned over the desk. "Well?"

It was very warm next to the big glowing stove. Karl felt like taking his shoes off and letting his feet bake on the lid. That and some good strong coffee would be heaven.

"What's up?" Al asked. "Who was that?"

"Denver Penitentiary. Guy named Bobby Lee escaped, and he's probably headed down here." Why did I say it? he thought. Why did I tell him? If I'd kept it to myself, we could've spent the whole afternoon here.

"Is that so?" Al said eagerly.

He's a good-looking kid, Karl decided. Good healthy teeth and bright yellow hair. His wife must love him very much. But why did she let him take a job like this? He should be out on a farm somewhere or working in the meatpacking line. But no. To Al this is glamor, this is excitement. This is law enforcement the way it happened in films and on television.

"How much?"

Karl looked up. "How much what?"

"Ammo." Al was unlocking the padlock on the armory closet.

Karl could see himself, thirty years ago, itching to get inside the closet while old Ben hung back and chuckled. Ben had probably dreamed of putting his stockinged feet on the stove and wished it was spring and the trout season. And Karl realized he had never faced real danger very often. Drunks and poachers – for the most part. Men who escaped from the penitentiary and carried Colt .45s hadn't been his type of chore. "Take the two Enfield .38s," he said, finally. "And the carbine." He knew Al wanted to take that. "Get plenty of ammo."

Al moved into the closet. When he came out his arms were full.

Why do we have to go? Karl thought. Let Bobby Lee drive his old Dodge through the hills and around the mountains. What harm could he do on a snowy afternoon with a blizzard coming up? Everybody is inside. Only the children are out on a day like this, and what would Bobby Lee want with a school kid?

"Should I load the stuff?" Al asked.

Karl stood up slowly. "Yeah, load it."

"What are you going to do?"

"Check the car." He put on his heavy woolen coat and picked up his boots.

"The car's okay. It was swell coming in this morning."

"Can't tell with that battery. I better check it."

Al shrugged and broke one of the revolvers open.

Karl went down the stairs to the street. He knew there wouldn't be anything wrong with the battery. You could let that car sit for a week in ten-below weather and it would turn over the first time you tried the ignition. No, the battery would be all right. He went outside into the driving wind. But checking the battery wasted time, it let minutes slip by while Bobby Lee hurried through the town or skirted it completely.

He went to the alleyway and got in the old touring car. He sat there on the torn upholstery, staring at his reflection in the windshield. The gray hair didn't prove his age. It was the neck, the wrinkled, sagging skin right under the chin that gave it away. But his appearance didn't matter to him. It was the change that old age made in his mind that counted. It made him afraid of snow, and wind, and grim lonely men who drove down from Denver. He thought suddenly, I retire in three weeks. Just three weeks.

He looked at the rear-view mirror. There was a tiny pair of white baby shoes dangling from it, attached by a string. Damn that Al, he thought. I let him use the car and right away he thinks it's his. If only I was alone on this thing. If only I didn't have *him* breathing down my neck, asking me about ammo and the other stuff.

Then he stared at the ignition key. Al had left it there in the dashboard that morning. Karl took it out and bounced it in his palm. All he had to do was open the window and throw it far, far away into a snow bank. The duplicate key was at his house, and they could never get transportation back there. They'd have to curse and fret about somebody's carelessness and spend the rest of the day upstairs in the office. Back at the stove. With coffee, maybe.

"Karl." It was Al's voice.

Karl looked around. Al had his face pressed to the car window, his open mouth clouding the glass. "Mrs. Hunter on Lakeridge Road. She just called. I think she saw that guy."

"What kind of car?"

"Gray Dodge sedan. We better hurry."

Karl moved over on the seat. "Yeah," he said. "Go back and get the stuff." He slid the key into the ignition.

They drove through the main shopping district, a frozen huddle of stores and low buildings. Children were sledding on some of the hills. They flashed by the car, swerving dangerously near the spinning wheels. "Crazy kids," said Al. Karl said nothing.

They moved slowly on the back roads, past white fields and the long silver river that stretched to the mountains. An old snow plow was trying to clear a path on the road to the Cooper hospital. The top of a telephone pole hung loose, supported by its wires.

"You're going awful slow," Al said.

"I know. You don't take fool chances on a day like this."

"Yeah, but you could go a *little* faster."

"If we were smart, we wouldn't have come at all."

Al looked at him, puzzled. "Then who would get this guy?"

Karl grunted. The wheels slipped, then caught, on an icy rise.

"Awful slow," Al complained. "That woman said to hurry."

"For God's sake!" Karl cried. "You want us to have an accident?" He hated to drive in snow. There was pressure every second, the chance of skidding off the road. "You want us to wind up dead?"

Al was silent for a moment, then he asked, "This guy a killer?"

"Yeah."

"Who'd he get?"

Karl fiddled with the heater. "Ted Wagner's son and his son's wife. Lee tried to break into their farmhouse. He killed them both. Among others."

Al felt the barrel of the carbine. "Happened right here in town?"

"Two miles past the drive-in."

Al was quiet for a few minutes. "I guess you've killed a lot of guys," he said suddenly.

"I never killed anybody." He wants me to play the hero. Well, I won't do it.

"I wonder how it feels? I mean, what's it like when you kill somebody?"

"Shut up, Al. You don't talk about those kinds of things." His hands trembled on the wheel. It's the cold, he told himself.

"I'm sorry," Al said. "I know what you mean."

"That's all right." His head felt warm. I'm getting a cold, he thought, just what I need. I should have stayed back at the office. In this weather I can catch a sore throat and then pneumonia. And the roads. Suppose they *did* have an accident? What would the town care?

"That's her place," said Al. "Right there." He pointed to a big house sitting off the road.

What would the town care? He had never thought of it that way.

"Hey! Slow down! This is the place."

He pulled into the narrow drive. A woman was waving from the porch.

"Better pull up to where she is," Al said. "She'll soak her feet coming down here."

"Let her walk," Karl said. "She's no invalid, is she?"

Al opened the door. "What's wrong with you?"

"Nothing. I just feel lousy. Sick." Be concerned, he thought. Take pity on an old man. You can take care of me, help me point my gun at Bobby Lee.

The woman came trudging over to the car. She was tall and lean. She wore a long leather coat and a bandanna. "Sheriff?"

"You the woman that called?"

"Yes, I am." The wind tore at her bandanna. "He was on the other side of those trees, where the road goes by. His car must have stalled. I heard about him on the radio."

"Where'd he go?"

"He went into the forest there. There's a couple of cabins at the back, if you go far enough. Used to be the Pine Motel."

"I know," Karl said impatiently. "Is that all the information you got?"

The woman frowned at him. "Well, yes. I heard on the radio that –"

"Sure!" Karl cried. "You report having any knowledge of his whereabouts, but *we're* supposed to get him. That's nice, isn't it?"

"Why, what d'you mean? It's your job. You get paid."

"Suppose that's not enough? Suppose we don't want to do it?"

The woman opened her mouth and looked at Al.

"What's wrong with you, Karl?" Al said. "He don't feel too good," he said to the woman. "You got a husband, ma'am?"

"He works for the railroad. He won't be back till seven or eight."

"Anybody else with you?" Al asked.

"My boy. He's fourteen."

"Lock yourselves in. Don't answer the door for nobody. I think maybe we'll use your phone now."

Karl laughed. "What good's a phone? You want help?"

"Sure. If we *know* he's in those woods…"

"Who are you going to get? Nobody'd come out here. This is our show, Al-boy." He felt pleased with himself for letting Al know that. Al might have been confused on that point.

"Ma'am," Al said, "you better get back in your house."

"You want me to call somebody for you?"

Al didn't look at Karl. "No."

Karl rubbed his hands together, feeling the cold get inside his gloves and under his coat.

"Go back in the house, ma'am," Al said.

The woman backed away slowly, looking at Karl, and went up to the porch. A young boy leaned over the railing to stare at them.

"Stupid kid," Karl growled under his breath.

Al gripped him by the arm. "What's up with you, Karl? Are you really sick?"

"What do you mean?" He *knows*. All right, Karl thought, let *him* play the hero. I'll stay in the car, and he can be brave under the trees. Too bad his wife isn't here to watch and clap for him.

"Look, Al, you haven't got much experience at this kind of thing."

"Do you?"

No, Karl thought, no, I don't. "Damn it," he said, "I know how to hunt. It's the same thing. You got to be careful."

"Let's go," Al said.

"Go where?"

Al flushed. "After Lee."

He's crazy, really crazy, Karl thought. He wants to walk out there with his carbine. Doesn't he realize that Lee's waiting, that he'd like nothing better than two guys coming in under the bare open trees?

"Come on," Al said firmly.

Karl decided that this would be easier for Lee than the time he had shot Wagner and his wife. Lee had to work for those deaths, had to grope in the dark.

"Al," he said suddenly, "this is Lakeridge Road, isn't it?"

Al looked at him queerly. "Yeah. Why?"

"We've got help!" Karl cried. "We've got somebody!"

"Who?"

"Ted Wagner. He's a huntsman, one of the best. Lee was the man who killed his son."

"You think he'll help us?"

"He will. Take my word for it." He didn't tell Al the part Ted Wagner had played in tracking Lee down the first time. He had given them blankets and lanterns, food and horses. They had been treated like nobility when they searched those woods outside of Cooper. Karl remembered clearly how Wagner had looked that night. He remembered the gray eyes in the long hard face, glowing with hatred. But Lee had surrendered in the early morning, and Wagner never had a chance to use his fine English rifle.

"I'm going down there," he said to Al.

"Where?"

"Wagner's. It's about a half-mile down the road. We need him."

Al looked at the slanting snow and the sky. "If you're sick, maybe I —"

"No. Stay here by the car. I'll be back with him in no time. He'll love it."

"Love it?"

Karl patted his shoulder. "Now stay here. Twenty minutes, that's all I'll be." He lumbered onto the road. He could hear Al's voice in the wind, calling something after him.

It was bad going. Some of the drifts were hip-deep; he felt the wet snow on his calves, leaking down his ankles inside his boots. All he saw was gray sky and trees and the snow. I'll catch pneumonia, he thought. But even that was better than one of Bobby Lee's bullets. Anything was better than that.

He suddenly thought of his wife resting safe and deep under an old stone in the Cooper churchyard. What would *she* say? Don't be a fool, Karl, that's what she'd say. You're pushing sixty and it's high time you got out from under. Tell them that's all, tell them to let Al take over. If you go easy, treat your body right, maybe you've got another ten years of hunting and fishing left.

But he knew that wasn't all she would say, knowing her as he did. Get *this* one over with, she'd say. Finish *this* one up. And he couldn't.

The Wagner house suddenly appeared. He hadn't realized he was this close. He stumbled across the big front lawn, through expensive walls of shrubs and hedges. There were pillars on the wide veranda. He thumped on the front door, shivering now.

The door opened and a manservant looked out.

"Is Mr. Wagner home?" Karl mumbled.

"Yes, sir, but..."

"Who is it, Arthur?" A man stood in the deep hallway shadows. He came closer slowly, and Karl recognized the tanned face and the hard body. He felt relief at once.

Wagner looked at him. "You were one of us on the..."

"The Lee business." He tried to smile, but his face felt like it was cracking. "You've got a good memory, sir."

"What are you doing out on a day like this?"

"Lee escaped from prison. He's wounded. We think he's in a patch of woods a little ways off."

Wagner placed his hands carefully in the pocket of his dressing gown. "Is that so? Hurt bad?"

"I don't know. I don't think so. He's got a .45 with him." A long chill flowed through his body, and he steadied himself with a hand against the wall. Wagner didn't say anything.

"Mr. Wagner," he began awkwardly. "I was wondering..."

"Yes?"

He couldn't think. It was as if both his body and his mind were frozen. He tried to stammer it out, but he couldn't. Wagner's face seemed to draw nearer.

"You're asking me to come with you?"

"Yes."

The tall man frowned. "No, that's out of the question. I can't. I'm sorry."

He couldn't believe his ears. "But...but before?"

"It was different then. I was fresh; I was angry. I talked myself into thinking it was my duty. But now? No."

"He was your son," Karl said, and felt anger spread inside him.

"I know, but this is not my responsibility, don't you see? It was their job before, too. Sometimes I'm glad he surrendered like he did."

"Don't you care?" Karl said. He was bewildered. He stared through a wide arch into a big, cheerful room. There was an older woman and a young girl sitting inside. A brick fireplace crackled with flames.

"Of course I care," Wagner said. "But it's not my job. It's yours."

"Mine?" Sure, it's mine, he thought. Hand it to me so you can go back in that warm room with your family. "So you're not going to come with me?"

"I'm sorry."

Suddenly he didn't care what he said. "What's the matter? Afraid?"

Wagner was a long time in answering. He smiled coldly. "Are

you?"

Karl was choked with anger. He opened the door and strode out on the veranda.

"Listen," Wagner called, "would you like a drink or something?"

"No," Karl shouted from the lawn. His voice was shrill. "I don't want anything." He plowed through the snow to the road and curved his shoulders against the wind. Who cares if I go after him? he thought. The woman who called in doesn't. Wagner and his family don't. The town doesn't care. Only Al, who thinks it's his duty. Al, who sees too many movies and watches too many television shows.

He had chills again, but he was glad that the way he felt was right. Thirty years in forests, and drunk tanks, and the old brick jail. But from now on, no more. He had to save what he had left for spring streams and that little cabin of his near Larkspur. He didn't care what Al said. Let Al call him a coward. So what? He'd go back to that car, get in, and drive home. And if Al wanted to stay there and prowl around for Bobby Lee, well, that was all right, too.

He saw the car up ahead. He felt like releasing himself by shooting, by laughing. He was free, and the hell with what Al thought.

When he made it to the car, bucking the wind, his head down, he pulled open the front door and slid halfway in. "Al..." he began. But Al wasn't there; the old car was empty. The carbine was gone, too.

"You fool!" he cried. He could see the tracks leading away across the field and into the blurred grove of trees. My God, that idiot! By himself, no less.

And then he felt something, something he didn't want, something he fought against. An irritating tug of the old responsibility. Not much. And not for the town. But responsibility for a green kid who carried a snapshot in his wallet and had a young pregnant wife at home.

He grabbed one of the guns and scrambled out into the snow. The tracks led straight into the tall, snow-heavy trees. He couldn't see anything in there except a white darkness and a windy tunnel of trunks. He threw away his red woolen scarf; it would be too easy to spot.

He went in under the trees. The gun barrel-down in his hand. The tracks, already half obscured by now, led straight ahead. He could still go back. He could start the car and drive home, call Ed Gruen and tell him that Al went alone. No. he *had* to find out where Al had gone, whether he had found Bobby Lee. God, he prayed that he hadn't. Lee knew what to do in a given situation. He knew how to double back on a trail, how to build and disguise a lean-to that not even a professional huntsman could spot. Through a clearing, just ahead of him, Karl made out an abandoned gray Dodge sedan.

He began to run. The old Pine Motel and a road that curved out to the highway were somewhere ahead. Then it appeared, a huge flat clearing that had once been an auto court, and the wind-haunted remains of ten log cabins. He fell on the ground and pressed his face to the snow. He couldn't feel anything anymore; his body was insensitive. He looked out into the misty clearing. There was a cabin not more than twenty feet away. He wasn't sure, but it seemed as if the tracks led straight to it. He peered hard and he thought he saw that the door was hanging open.

He shifted and crawled through the snowdrift, inching his way around behind the cabin. Then he stood up slowly.

There was a terrific gunshot blast. It hammered at the ruined walls, at the trunks, seemed to fill the winter sky. He was moving almost before he realized that it had come from the cabin.

He ran and stumbled into the clearing, heading for the door with his gun raised. He clattered up the steps, shouldered the door, and ducked inside, crouched low. "Lee!" he screamed. "Lee!"

There was no roof on the cabin. The snow fell gently on the rotting floor. A man lay on his stomach near the door. He wore a green hunting cap and gripped a .45 in one still hand.

Karl came over and looked down at the face. It was Bobby Lee and he was dead. Karl turned slowly and saw Al standing on the other side of the room. "Al! What happened?"

Al leaned his smoking carbine against the wall. His face looked blue from the cold. "I found him in here about five minutes ago. He was dead. Loss of blood from the hip wound, I guess."

"But the gunshot just now. What was it?"

Al didn't say anything.

"The gunshot. What was it?" He walked over to Al and stared into his face.

"I saw you out there in the snow," Al said softly. "That shooting – well, I did it on an impulse. I wanted to see if…" He let his voice trail off.

Karl lowered his eyes. He said nothing, but he felt a subdued relief. This was the last chore. Thirty years, and now he was through. "I'm quitting tomorrow," he said.

"Yeah, I figured."

"It feels good to say that, Al. Someday you'll know what I mean."

They went out together and trudged their way back to the car. It was snowing harder.

MEMORY GAME

"All right now, give this a try, Mr. Perkins. What's the altitude of Mount Everest?"

Mr. Leroy Perkins touched his glass to the bar and observed the neat, wet circle it made. "Twenty-nine thousand, one hundred and forty-one feet," he said.

"Check it, Sam," said one of the men at the bar.

The bartender paged through a copy of the *World Almanac.* "Yep," he said. "He's right."

"Another round, Leroy?" Jake Underwood asked. Jake was a shriveled little man, Mr. Perkins' neighbor, and the two of them drank together every night.

"I don't think so, Jake. We've already had our three." Mr. Perkins studied his reflection in the bar mirror. It looked pleasantly blurred to him, a signal that he had had enough.

Sam flipped to another page. "What was Lou Gehrig's batting average in 1925?"

Mr. Perkins yawned. A glance at his pocket watch showed him it was already eleven. Alice was probably waiting for him to appear under the streetlight. Let her wait, he thought with sudden anger. I'm a man; I can come home when I damn well please. "That'd be .295," he told Sam.

"Yeah," said someone else. "But how many consecutive games did he play?"

"Two thousand, one hundred and three."

"That's what it says in here," Sam said. "What a memory."

Mr. Perkins curled his thin lips in a smile. Yes, what a memory. Sometimes he even amazed himself. Ever since he was a boy he had used the infinite quantity of his mind to amuse and astonish others. It was as if nature had compensated for his fragile body, his poor heath, his myopic vision. Occasionally, he thought it a shame that he had not used his memory professionally, rather than just as a hobby. But Alice would have forbidden it. He could imagine her scalding remarks: "Are you crazy? What do you want people to think you are – a freak?"

"Come on, let's have another one," Jake whispered. "Alice won't be able to tell the difference."

"Afraid not, Jake. Three a night. That's my limit."

"You've had more'n that some nights."

"Only twice before, both last year. And then I only had four."

Jake grunted and slid off his stool. "Well, if you're not gonna drink with me, I may as well go on home. Clara will give me the dickens if I'm not back by eleven-thirty."

Mr. Perkins didn't look at him. They usually left the bar together every night. But on this particular evening, with vague rebellion in his blood, he wanted to stay. Let Alice wonder for a change. Let her – "See you tomorrow, Jake."

"Okay, Leroy. Good night."

Jake moved through the door and some of the other men, as if following an example, finished their drinks and began to leave.

Mr. Perkins' eyes met those of the drunk standing alone at the end of the bar. The man was resting his unshaven chin on the lip of his glass. Mr. Perkins knew the man had been there, off and on, for the past month. Just sitting there, evening after evening, ordering cheap bourbon and listening to them play the memory game.

Sam began wiping the counter. "Maybe you'd better go home, Mr. Perkins," he said with a half-grin. "Alice will give you hell."

"No, she won't," he said loudly. He noted that the alcohol had enriched the timbre of his voice, added cubits to his courage. "She'll get a good beating if she so much as opens her mouth."

The bartender turned, but Mr. Perkins caught his smile in the mirror. He's laughing at me, he thought. What a fool he must think I am! In here every night with Jake playing the game, and then talking about Alice or Clara. Two henpecked fools distilling bravery from a bottle.

Blushing, Mr. Perkins rose from the stool and put his tip on the counter. "Well, I'll be going. 'Night, Sam."

"'Night, Mr. Perkins. Don't run *too* fast." Sam laughed and winked at the drunk.

Mr. Perkins made his way to the door. He should have walked home with Jake; it would have saved him this embarrassment. As he was about to go out a voice called to him softly. "Mr. Perkins?"

Startled, Mr. Perkins turned and saw the drunk approaching him. "And what do you want?"

The drunk motioned to a private booth. "Sit down. I want to talk to you."

Probably wants a loan or a handout of some kind, Mr. Perkins thought. "I really have to go," he said. "My wife's expecting me."

"This won't take long."

Mr. Perkins stared at him. The man was young, twenty-eight or twenty-nine, with a moist dissipated face. The astonishing fact was that he didn't look a bit drunk. His eyes were perfectly clear.

"Sit down." The man slid into the booth.

Mr. Perkins obeyed, timorously. "W-what is it?"

"I been comin' in here pretty regularly lately. You seen me?"

Mr. Perkins nodded. Behind him, he could hear Sam closing up for the night.

"I watched that game you play with the bartender. You're great. How come you remember all that stuff?"

"I – don't know. I just don't forget things I hear or read."

Some of the overhead lights went out, throwing an island of shadow across the booth. "I'll bet you do a lot of reading," the man said. "It keeps Alice off your back, huh? Keeps you from thinking about her."

Mr. Perkins didn't answer.

"Listen, I keep hearin' you complain about your wife to that buddy of yours. About what a hard time she gives you. You wanna get rid of her?"

The calm words, so casually spoken, stunned Mr. Perkins. His back stiffened; he could feel the tingle of blood rushing to his face. "W-what did you say?" he stammered.

"I said, do you wanna get rid of her? Permanently."

Mr. Perkins groped to his feet. "I really must go."

"You didn't answer my question."

"I – I didn't hear what you said."

"Yes, you did."

"We're closing up, Mr. Perkins," Sam called. "You want Alice to come looking for you, do you?"

Mr. Perkins moved out of the booth and went quickly toward the door.

"Hey!" the man called. "Come back for a minute."

Mr. Perkins slammed the door and hurried off down the empty street. I should have gone home with Jake, he thought. Then none of this would have happened. He tried to put it out of his mind, but the man's question kept repeating itself. *Do you wanna get rid of her? Permanently.* He tried to blot it out, but he was unable to. It was still buzzing in his mind when he arrived home and found Alice waiting for him.

The following evening after dinner, Mr. Perkins sat exhausted in the living room. It was Saturday and Alice had made him paint the basement. His bones ached from climbing up and down the stepladder, stretching his body at uncomfortable angles over the damp walls. He dreaded Sunday morning, for after church he would be sent down to finish the job.

He went quietly to the closet and took his coat and hat. It would be good to snuggle into Sam's and look down on the world from a high stool.

"Leroy?" Alice had come in from the porch. "Where are you going?"

"Just down to Sam's."

"Not tonight. You have to finish the cellar."

"Alice," he began to protest, "I have all day tomorrow to –"

"Tomorrow we've got that planting in the garden. So just take off your coat and go downstairs."

Mr. Perkins sighed deeply. It was useless to argue with her. He had tried that only five times in his married life, and the results had been painful. He put his coat and hat back in the closet and slammed the door.

"Stop slamming things!" Alice called from the kitchen.

Mr. Perkins went down the stairs into the basement. A dim bulb illuminated the half-finished walls, the sticky gallon cans of fresh paint. His overalls lay on the cement floor like a collapsed tent. They smelled of turpentine and perspiration. He felt slightly dizzy from the aroma of mustiness and raw paint. No, it was an impossibility. He couldn't manage painting the walls tonight.

He tiptoed to the door that led to the backyard and listened for a few moments. Alice was upstairs, running water in the sink. Carefully, he opened the door and drifted along the side of the house. He wore no coat and the evening wind chilled his face and bare arms. He ducked under the kitchen window, heard Alice humming to herself. Then he edged around the garage and walked out to the street.

"Hey, Leroy."

Mr. Perkins whirled, his heart pounding. Then he relaxed; the voice had come from Jake Underwood's home. He could see the tip of Jake's cigar glowing over a row of geraniums on the porch railing. "I'll be right with you, Jake," he called.

"How far is the Rio de la Plata River from Buenos Aires?"

"Approximately one hundred and seventy-five miles," said Mr. Perkins. He looked across at the drunk and saw that the man was watching him. The unblinking careful stare unnerved him.

Sam was smiling. "Right on the button. Bull's eye. Don't you ever miss?"

"I guess not." He glanced at Jake, who was resting his head on the bar, snoring softly. Too much Scotch, Mr. Perkins thought. He drinks more every night. Poor old guy.

When he looked up, the drunk had sat down beside him. Sam was at the far end of the bar, serving a customer.

"Did you think over what I said?"

Mr. Perkins was silent for a while. Then he nodded.

"Well?"

"Well what?" Mr. Perkins watched Jake, but the old man was still sleeping.

"It'll cost you money," the drunk said.

"How much?"

"A thousand bucks. Cash."

Mr. Perkins finished his drink. "That's – that's out of the question. I couldn't get my hands on that much."

"Eight hundred."

"Still too much."

Jake began to stir.

The drunk seemed restless. "Listen, we can't talk here. Meet me outside in ten minutes. Without your friend." He went to the door, opened it, and walked out to the street.

"How 'bout another round, Leroy?" Jake said thickly.

"I've had my three, Jake. Sorry. Besides, I'm leaving in a few minutes. Have to go back and finish some painting."

"At this hour?" Jake said.

"That's right."

Mr. Perkins waited a full ten minutes, then said goodnight to Jake and Sam.

The drunk was standing against the side of the building when he came out. "Let's grab a bus, Perkins. I don't want anybody seein' us walkin' together on the street."

They took a southbound bus and the drunk let Mr. Perkins pay the fare. The bus was reasonably empty and they took double seats in the rear.

"Now let's get down to business," said the drunk. "How much can you afford?"

"Five hundred dollars," said Mr. Perkins.

"You're crazy! You think I want to risk the electric chair for that?"

"But that's all I can possible scrape up."

The drunk stared through the window. The bus was entering the suburbs, a vast area of new development houses. Abruptly he turned back to Mr. Perkins. "How much jewelry does your wife have?"

"Three pieces, heirlooms. Why?"

The drunk propped his feet on the seat in front of him. "How much are they worth?"

"Well, we had them appraised a few months ago."

"You happen to remember how much –"

"Four hundred and eighty dollars," Mr. Perkins said.

The drunk laughed. "I forgot about the way you remember things. Okay, I'll take the jewelry. Plus the five hundred. That way the cops'll think it's a robbery."

"Oh, I see," Mr. Perkins said.

"When do you want it to happen?"

"Happen?" Mr. Perkins was puzzled for a moment. It all didn't seem quite real. But this request for a date suddenly gave it actuality. "Let's say, well, let's say this coming Monday night. Jake and I can go down to Sam's while you – well, you know."

"Good idea. If the police check you'll have a perfect alibi. Hell, you've been going down there every night for – how long now?"

"Three years, two months, and fifteen days," said Mr. Perkins.

"Yeah. Well, as I say, it's a perfect alibi. When can you have the five hundred?"

"I can take it out of the bank Monday morning."

"Good. Where can you leave it for me?"

"It'll be in the pocket of a pair of overalls in the basement. Alice will never look there."

The drunk rose and stood swaying over the seat. "Here's where I get off. I'll give you my phone number in case anything goes wrong."

Mr. Perkins listened to the drunk's telephone number, amazed by the audacity of the thing he had just done. The bargain was made. Everything was simple. A conference on a dream-like bus and soon, Monday night to be exact, Alice would cease to be a burden.

"Any questions?"

"No." Mr. Perkins dug into his watch pocket. "Here, I'll give you my house key."

"I don't want it. This has to look legitimate. I'll jimmy a window."

"Sorry," said Mr. Perkins. "I guess I'm an amateur at these things."

The drunk smiled. "Just make sure to leave your place at nine o'clock Monday night and go straight to Sam's. I'll leave mine at nine-thirty and be at your house about ten. Right?"

Mr. Perkins nodded. He was about to extend his hand, but he suddenly realized it wouldn't be the proper thing to do. He watched as the drunk swung up the aisle and left the bus.

The following night, after dinner, Mr. Perkins' telephone rang.

He was stretched out on the bed, recuperating from the siege of painting that morning. The thought occurred to him while Alice's high-heels tapped downstairs in the living room, that perhaps *he* was calling. Panic stricken, he shouted, "I've got it, Alice!" and grabbed for the phone. "Hello?"

"Perkins?" It was the drunk's voice, no mistake about that.

"You shouldn't have called here," Mr. Perkins whispered.

"What?"

"I said you shouldn't have called me here. There's an extension downstairs and my wife might listen in."

There was a short pause. "Well? What do you think? Is she listening or not?"

"I don't think so."

"Okay. I'll make this short. I want more money."

Mr. Perkins dabbed at his wet forehead. "But I told you –"

"Another two hundred. You can spare it."

"But I can't! I thought we had this all straightened out."

"Seven hundred in cash, Perkins. Agreed? After all, I can't get much for your jewelry. And I'm taking a big chance."

Mr. Perkins darted over to the bedroom door and closed it. Then he said angrily into the phone, "All right. But this is a dirty trick to play."

"Leave the money in the overalls, right?"

"Right."

"Then tomorrow night it is. 'Bye." The connection snapped off.

Mr. Perkins replaced the receiver and dropped back on the bed. His heart was pounding, his hands were ice-cold. Suppose something went wrong? he thought. Suppose Alice decided to visit a friend and wasn't home when the drunk broke in? No, he refused to think about it. Besides, he would be insured by a perfect alibi. Monday night would be like any other night: he would eat dinner, walk leisurely to Sam's, have a few drinks and play the memory game…He rolled over and tried to go to sleep.

"Here's one for you, Mr. Perkins," Sam said. "How many votes did Buchanan get against Fremont and Fillmore in 1856?"

Mr. Perkins took a slow sip of his drink and looked around at the others. They had seen his exhibition every night for years, but it still fascinated them. "One million, eight hundred and eighty-eight thousand, one hundred and sixty-nine," he said, finally.

Sam snapped the encyclopedia closed. "Right," he said with a jerk of his head.

The others shouted approval, a few slapping Mr. Perkins on the back. He smiled at them and then stole a look at his watch. It was almost nine-fifteen. At the half-hour mark the drunk would be leaving to do his special work.

Mr. Perkins took his fresh drink and tinkled the ice with his swizzle stick. Tonight he would have more than three. He felt buoyant. Sam had opened the doors and windows and the fresh breeze brought the smell of grass and trees into the stale room. It would feel wonderful to be free, Mr. Perkins thought. Like a spring kite cut loose. He would sell the house and rent a bachelor's apartment near the park. Maybe he'd buy himself a little car, one of those economical sports models. He had certainly fooled the drunk. There was still two thousand dollars left in his savings account, ready to be taken out the day after Alice's funeral. Maybe he'd quit his job at the insurance company and go on the stage with a magic memory act. It was possible, it was possible...

He took a strong pull of the drink and looked up. His friend Jake had come in. Leroy!" he said. "Leroy!"

"What is it, Jake?"

Jake squeezed in beside him, his small face puckered with excitement. "Listen to this —"

"Calm down. Listen to what?"

"I looked over at your house when I left tonight. Somethin's going on."

"What are you talking about?"

"There were cops there!" Jake said. "Alice opened the door and let them in. And then the other cop drove their car out of sight. They're waitin' for somebody, Leroy. It must be that."

Mr. Perkins dug his nails into the wood of the bar. Alice must have heard the phone call on the extension! She had the police waiting and they would catch the drunk. It would be all over, finished. The drunk would squeal on him and they'd put him in prison. Alice would be fiendishly happy; she would love to see him behind bars.

But wait! He looked at his watch. It was only nine-twenty. The drunk still had ten minutes before he left his home. There was plenty of time to call him, to warn him not to leave.

Mr. Perkins sprang from the stool, upsetting it. "Hey!" Sam yelled.

The telephone booth was next to the doorway. It was empty. Smiling, Mr. Perkins pulled the door open and slid into the cubicle. He reached into his trouser pockets and removed his change. Ahh, the luck! he thought. There were three shiny dimes on his palm. He dropped one into the slot and listened to the dial tone. Then he lifted his hand and shot his finger toward the dial. And then he stopped, his stomach suddenly dead, his thoughts petrified.

He had forgotten the telephone number.

THE JOAN CLUB

In the cab, Joe Dennis put his arm around her and she leaned into him deftly and precisely. Her ear was at his mouth, white and fragile in the dimness, and he kissed it. "You're just about the most beautiful girl who ever lived," he said. He meant it; he was perfectly sober.

Joan reacted as she always did to a compliment. Her head inclined a fraction in acknowledgement, but the lovely face remained expressionless, the blue eyes revealed nothing.

They left the cab at her building. The elevator lifted them toward her floor, then the door rolled open and they walked the short corridor to her door. He inserted the key. "Open sesame," he said lightly, but the words sounded monumentally inane in his ears. The door swung back, revealing her apartment in the glow of one muted lamp. She took the key from the door and dropped it into her purse.

"You're not coming in, you know," she said.

"I'm not what?"

She put a gloved hand on his arm. "Joe, it's been a nice evening. I want to thank you. But don't call me again. It won't do you any good."

"Well, now, wait a minute –" he began.

"No. It's over, Joe. Let it stay that way." She smiled at him, and the door closed. He stayed in the hallway for a long time before he pressed the elevator button.

On Monday morning he unlocked his mail slot in the lobby and opened the one envelope inside. A small white card fell out:

You are invited to the weekly meeting of
THE JOAN CLUB
One o'clock today.
Cocktails and Luncheon.
The Park House

He studied the card, thoroughly confused, then slipped it into his billfold and hurried out to catch his bus.

The Park House fronted on the park, its windows draped and secluded against the afternoon heat and the spray of nearby fountains. The manager greeted Joe with a smile. "Mr. Dennis? That table in the rear, sir." Joe's eyes followed the man's finger to a group of men seated in a far corner by the windows. He crossed the room, past lunching couples, and stopped at the table. "Is this…?"

"It is, Mr. Dennis," said one of the men. He stood up. "Glad you came. I'm Hank Robard. Let me introduce our little klatsch."

Bewildered, Joe shook hands with a Mr. Ed Dougherty, a Mr. Guy Pryor and a Mr. Lew Jackson. They all regarded him with faint amusement. Robard seemed to be in charge. He signaled a waiter and ordered drinks. "A double for you, eh, Joe?" he said. "You can probably use one after the other night."

Joe was beginning to feel angry. "Look, Mr. Robard, I may be abnormally slow, but I don't get this. And I'm not sure I like it."

"Don't draw it out," said Pryor. "Tell him about us."

Robard chuckled. "All right." He turned to Joe. "Mr. Dennis, are we correct in assuming you were shot down Saturday evening by a lovely, cold-blooded young thing named Joan?"

"I don't think it's any of your business," said Joe.

"She ditched *all* of us," said the man named Jackson.

Joe was stunned. "You mean all of you dated Joan?"

"Not at the same time, of course," said Pryor.

"And each of us found himself in your position, Mr. Dennis," said Robard. "The door was closed, so to speak, in all of our faces." The drinks had come and he raised a toast. "The usual toast," he said. "To Joan and the man who…" He grinned. "Well, cheers." They drank.

"So," said Robard, "that's it, Dennis. We're the most exclusive club in the city."

"How did you know about me?" asked Joe.

"I live in her apartment building," said Robard. "That's how I met her. Pryor here rooms with me. I dated her, got my fingers burned, then he took her out. Ditto with him. So we began to keep tabs on her dates, just for the hell of it. Jackson was next. Then Dougherty."

"Then me?" said Joe.

"Then you," said Robard. "But now to business. The name of the next victim is Raymond Walsh."

"How did you find out?" asked Joe.

"Simplicity itself. I saw him with Joan, so I met him in the lobby and bought him a drink."

"Did he talk about her?" Joe asked.

"No. Very secretive. He thinks he has something good, so he doesn't want to spread it around."

"Raymond Walsh," Pryor said.

"And then there were six," said Dougherty.

Joan turned her head from the pillow and looked at Ray Walsh. He was smoking a cigarette, eyes half closed. She put her arm around him. "I've never, never done this before," she said. "Do you realize that?"

Walsh removed her hand. He sat up in bed and looked at his watch. "I have to go now, Joan."

"No," she said. "I want you to stay until morning. I'll make breakfast."

He studied her for a moment, impassively. Then he got up and began putting on his shirt.

"You don't understand," she said. "You're the first man. They've never even come in here before."

"Why not?" He was pulling on his trousers.

"I haven't wanted them to. I've stopped them. They all wanted what I gave to you. I want you to stay. I'm in *love* with you."

She got out of bed as he gathered his coat. Her nude body was like living alabaster. "You're not really leaving, are you?"

"Yes."

"You'll call me, won't you?"

He opened the door. "I don't think so."

"Ray!" she called, but the door had closed.

On Monday morning, in her mailbox, she found an envelope addressed to her.

There was a white card inside:

You are invited to the weekly meeting of
THE RAYMOND CLUB
One o'clock today. Cocktails and
luncheon.
The Paris Café.

DEAR CORPUS DELICTI

Charles Lowe looked down at his wife. She lay on her side, the silk scarf knotted under her neck like a small, red flower. He held his hand near her mouth, but she had stopped breathing. Then he checked his watch – there was still plenty of time.

Moving carefully around her, he opened the French doors and stepped out on the flagged terrace. A light wind from the East River cooled him, dried the sweat on his forehead. He steadied himself against the glass door for a moment, then closed it behind him. On the edge of the terrace, near the railing, stood a row of flowerpots. They had been purchased by his wife, and every morning she gave them a ritual watering. Lowe picked one up, tested its weight, and moved back to the door. It took only a light, gentle tap to shatter one of the panels; the glass shards tinkled on the study floor.

Lowe returned the pot and went back into the apartment, leaving the French doors partly open. Now if he could find her purse everything would be ready. Where did she keep it? Married six years and he didn't even know.

He searched the study and the bedroom before finding it on the hall table. Good. Very good. It was now virtually perfect. The maid would come the following morning and find her body in the study. It would look like a simple case of robbery. A sneak thief had climbed up on the terrace and broken in. But Vivian had caught him and he had strangled her with her scarf. He had fled, taking her purse.

Lowe whistled softly and opened his wallet. The two airline tickets. The most important of all was still to come. He buttoned his tan raincoat, replaced the wallet, and stood at the door. Inside, in the darkened study, he could see his wife's outflung hand. The wedding band twinkled.

Lowe took a deep breath and left the apartment.

When he reached the street, he looked up toward the terrace. It was lost in darkness, impossible to see. He stepped into the street and hailed a cab. "Ninety-sixth and West End," he told the driver.

It was growing colder when the cab left him off. A thick river mist smudged the streetlights. Where the devil is she? he thought. I told her six on the dot.

He waited nervously under a hotel canopy, glancing at his watch. His wife had always been punctual; Sue was always late. His wife was quick and dependable, as meticulous as a man; Sue was slow and childishly helpless. He smiled suddenly and looked up. She was crossing the street, moving against the wind, her blonde hair blowing loose.

"Am I late?" she asked breathlessly.

"Yes, as usual. But it doesn't matter."

"I tried to get the early bus, but it didn't stop. I don't know –"

He put a finger on her lips. "It's all right. We've got plenty of time. So stop worrying."

He took her arm, guided her into the street. "Did you remember the glasses?" he asked.

"The glasses?"

"For God's sake, Sue, I *told* you a thousand times. Your sunglasses. Now we've got to –"

"But I have them," she said. "I thought you meant my reading glasses. I only wear those when I read."

Lowe shook his head, wearily. "Put them on."

He studied her in the dark spectacles. She resembled Vivian now – the small, well-formed figure, the blond hair. It was enough to fool a casual observer, and that was all that mattered.

"How do I look?" she said.

"Like my ex-wife."

Her lip trembled, but he couldn't see the eyes behind the glasses. "Charles. Did you –"

"We agreed not to talk about it. Remember?"

She nodded. He flagged a cab and helped her in. The driver had a Hungarian name and spoke broken English. Another lucky break, Lowe thought.

"Take us to Idlewild," he said. "As fast as you can."

Sue snuggled next to him; her hand groped over his. "Here," he said, handing her Vivian's purse.

"What's this?"

"You'll need it for identification at the airline desk. Now no more questions. I'll tell you what to do – step by step."

She laid her head on his shoulder, staring up at his face. "Maybe we shouldn't," she whispered. "Charles, it's a terrible thing. We –"

He bent down and kissed her. "We're committed," he said. "We have to go through with it. Now relax."

He put his arm around her and looked out over the highway. Traffic was sparse, but they were moving well under the speed limit. "Hurry it up," he said. "Faster."

Soon the buildings were behind. They moved through shopping centers and along boulevards. Overhead, a huge airliner droned by, its wing tips blinking.

"How much farther?" she whispered.

"A few more miles."

Minutes later they were on the periphery of the gigantic airport. There were more planes in the black sky, circling, climbing. "Let us off at the Trans-Continental Building," he told the driver.

He sat, relaxed but watchful as clumps of buildings rushed up in the windshield. The taxi swerved ahead of a line of cars, heading for the main entrance. Finally they stopped, skidding, at the entrance door. The driver looked back at them, smiling.

Lowe paid the fare and helped her out of the car. "I gave him a heavy tip," he said. "He'll remember us."

The airline terminal was brightly lit and crowded. Lowe stopped just inside the entrance and moved closer to her. "All right. It's up to you now."

"What?"

"Go over to the counter and check us in. If they ask for baggage tell them we're traveling without it."

Her eyes blinked at him. "But – but I don't know what to do. I never did this before."

"It's simple. The man will do all the work. Go ahead." He squeezed her arm and shoved her forward, feeling vaguely sorry for her. She looked back helplessly, then turned and hurried toward the counter.

Lowe glanced at the airline clock, checked it against his watch. They had thirty minutes until takeoff time. He took out a cigarette.

"Charles!" The voice cut sharply through the room. He looked up quickly. She was standing at the counter, her face white, staring at him. He felt that everyone in the room was watching.

"What is it?" he called.

"The tickets!"

He went quickly to the counter. The airline attendant was smiling.

"Oh, yes, I forgot to give them to you." He removed his wallet, his hands perfectly steady, and slid the two envelopes across the counter.

The attendant checked the tickets, phoned for confirmation, and handed Lowe a small card. "Give this to the hostess when you board. Thank you, sir. Enjoy your flight."

Lowe nodded and turned away. He grabbed Sue tightly by the arm and led her toward the lounge.

"Was I all right?"

"Fine. Just fine."

"Where are we going?"

"The lounge. We'd better have a drink. I think I need one."

They stood at the gate leading to the field. Lowe's two drinks had gone to his head; he felt sleepy and less excited. Sue's face was flushed, almost feverish.

"Charles," she said lightly. "I think I – I had a little too much…"

"That's all right. It's good for you." He put his arm around her waist. She seemed perfectly relaxed, weightless.

The crowd jostled them as the gate swung open. They walked out along the night runway following the airline attendant.

Lowe tightened his grip on her arm. "Do you know what to do?"

"I'm…not exactly sure."

"As soon as we get settled in our seats we'll begin to argue. Loud – so that everyone can hear. And you won't take it. In fact, you get up and leave."

"But what can we argue about?"

"It doesn't matter. I'll start it off. Just follow my lead."

A cold wind shook at them, carrying a little pocket of rain. Ahead, the long, silver airliner gleamed wet in the darkness.

"After you leave the plane," said Lowe, "what do you do then?"

"I take a taxi straight home. And I stay there all weekend."

"Right. And you don't call anyone. I'll be back on Monday. I'll try to come and see you."

"I want you to call me, Charles. Please. I don't know how I'll get through the weekend without hearing from you."

"I'll try."

They reached the boarding platform and Lowe helped her up the first step. It was beginning to rain now in heavy, blowing gusts. The hostess, standing at the door, gave them a professional smile.

"Nice weather," Lowe said wryly.

"Just over New York," the hostess said. "We'll be out of it as soon as we're airborne."

"Famous last words." He smiled at her and entered her cabin.

Sue was taking off her raincoat, her teeth chattering. "I think I caught a chill."

"Maybe you better keep your coat on." He held it open for her, and she slipped into it. "You take the aisle seat," he whispered.

They sat down in the deep, upholstered chairs. The second hostess came by and leaned over them. "We'll have some hot coffee right after takeoff," she said.

"Fine," Lowe said. "We can use it." He looked down the long, lit cabin. The plane was almost filled; people were standing in the aisles, hoisting overnight cases in the racks, ducking down into their warm seats. Rain beat on the windows, blurring the field.

"Charles," Sue said, "I'm frightened. I don't like flying in this kind of weather."

He looked at her coldly. "Always complaining. I'm getting sick and tired of it."

She glanced at him, hurt and surprised, before she realized what he was doing.

"You didn't want to come along in the first place," he continued loudly. "You don't want to do anything with me anymore."

"That's a lie!"

"Is it?" He watched an old man in the forward section turn to look at them. "The only thing you want from me is money. Out buying clothes, going to the theater – anything to stay away from home. You spend more time with your friends than with me!"

She began to cry. Excellent, he thought. Keep it up. Other people were watching.

"I thought we could take a trip together for a change, maybe get to know each other again. But you don't even want to come along!"

She stood up in the seat. "No, I don't," she said, sobbing. "And I'm not."

"Fine! Go home. Go to your friends. I don't particularly give a damn." He looked at her. "What are you waiting for?"

She hurried to the rear of the plane. Her voice was sharp and clear in the whole cabin. "I'm getting off."

"But ma'am," said the flight attendant, "we're almost ready to taxi."

"I don't care. Let me off!"

Lowe turned his face to the window. There were muffled words and more crying from the rear. The attendant had opened the door and was shouting something into the rain.

The hostess came over to his seat. "Mr. Lowe," she said softly. "Perhaps I could talk to her. Maybe –"

"No," he said bitterly. "If she wants to leave, fine. I don't care."

The hostess nodded somberly, and went away. Lowe looked through the window. They were wheeling the aluminum platform back to the door. It made a sharp sound as it connected to the body of the plane.

He watched as Sue came down the platform and huddled under the attendant's umbrella. She looked up at his window for a brief moment, her face streaked and lonely, then turned and went off.

Lowe rested his head against the soft cushion. Perfect. At least twenty passengers had seen Mrs. Vivian Lowe leave her husband in a rage and return to the terminal. From there the police would construct a rough timetable. She had gone back to the apartment, just in time to catch a thief breaking in. He had killed her and fled. And her husband? Where was he? Thousands of feet up in the sky, sulking over his wife's behavior. A perfect, perfect alibi.

The hostess, warm and sympathetic, was back at his side. "We'll have coffee in a few minutes, Mr. Lowe. Will you want some?"

"Yes," he said. "Lots of it."

The weekend was relaxing and uneventful. Lowe spent it at a hunting lodge a few miles from Montreal. He shared most of his time with some vacationing businessmen, playing bridge, fishing, and discussing politics over mellow Canadian whiskey. It was a shame that after two pleasant days of rest, he'd return to be told of his wife's unfortunate death.

During the flight back to New York, Lowe speculated on his new life. He'd be unencumbered, free to travel, relieved of his wife's financial drain. There was Sue, of course, but he could take his time with her. Eventually they'd be married. She was docile enough; she wouldn't be a burden.

He looked through the window. The plane was circling above Idlewild, beginning its long descent. The SAFETY BELTS sign glowed red. He smiled as the plane tipped imperceptibly forward.

Later, in the airport grill, he had a steak sandwich and a beer. He read a copy of the *Times* with his meal; there was no sense hurrying. He was surprised to find that very little had happened in the world during the past two days.

On the way back to the city he told the taxi driver to take his time. It was a long, leisurely ride with the sun on his face. "This is the way to do it," the driver said. "Everybody's always in such a hurry."

"They ought to learn to slow down," said Lowe expansively. "Take life easy."

The cab left him off in front of his apartment building. The doorman was talking on the phone. That's good, Lowe thought. I don't want any phony condolences from him. He took the self-service elevator to his floor and walked slowly down the hall.

"Mr. Lowe?"

He turned from the door, digging in his pocket for his key. "Yes?"

A slight, insignificant little man came and stood near the stairway. He came forward, holding his hat. "Lieutenant Fisher," he said, "Forty-fifth Precinct."

Lowe frowned. Well, here it comes, he thought. Let's hope I can react properly. "What can I do for you, Lieutenant?"

"It's, well, it's bad news, Mr. Lowe. We tried to contact you all weekend, but your office said you were out of town."

Lowe smiled. "Yes, I was in Montreal. Fishing trip. Doctor's orders." He looked down at the doormat. There was a slip of paper pushed under its edge. He bent down and picked it up.

"It's about your wife, Mr. Lowe. She – she was killed Friday night."

Lowe didn't look up at him. He stared at the slip of paper, his heart swelling against his chest. It was a scribbled note from the maid: "Mr. Lowe – my sister took sick so I couldn't come in. I will come Tuesday instead."

Lieutenant Fisher fingered his hat. "She was coming from the airport in a taxi. It crashed into a furniture truck…"

In a daze, Lowe turned the key in the lock, pushed the door open. Standing in the hallway, his eyes moved toward the study.

"We found her purse in the cab," Fisher continued, "and got her identification…"

Lowe felt faint. He stared at the outflung hand in the study doorway. The wedding band glinted in the light from the French doors.

"There'll be a few details," Fisher said. "It won't take long." He looked at Lowe's frozen face. "May I come in?"

WHO IS JESSICA?

M rs. Lenore Dunning woke up one night for no apparent reason and found it difficult to doze off again. The luminous clock on the dresser told her it was almost three and its loud, clear ticking disturbed her. Arthur, her husband, was turning restlessly in his sleep, and it seemed for a moment that he had said something. She listened. He rolled over on his back and muttered, "Jessica…Jessica…" Then he was quiet, deep in a dream that held him completely.

Mrs. Dunning was puzzled, but she finally fell asleep and by morning had forgotten the incident. The following night it happened again.

She was undressing for bed, combing her long, dark hair. Arthur had retired earlier in the evening and he was lying very still in the double bed. He suddenly turned over and began to whisper. Mrs. Dunning moved quickly from the mirror and stood over him. He was dream-talking, his lips slightly wet and open. She bent her head until her ear almost touched his mouth. "Jessica," he said, very distinctly. For a span of seconds, his face – after he mentioned the name – was perfectly content.

Mrs. Dunning did not sleep well that night. The next morning she rose before her husband and helped the maid set the breakfast table. Then she sat down and drank a cup of coffee, smoking nervously and thinking. Jessica. It would be a girl, of course, some new young thing that he was seeing. He had even gotten to the point where he was dreaming about her.

Oh, damn him! she thought, stubbing her cigarette into an ashtray. Damn him! She felt like crying, but the maid was there, and she managed to control herself.

Later, Arthur came down and joined her at the long table. He smiled at her and drank his orange juice. "How are we feeling this morning?" he asked.

Mrs. Dunning shook two pills from a bottle and washed them down with coffee. "A little better," she said.

The maid always set the paper at Arthur's elbow. He picked it up and snapped it open. "Maybe those new pills will do the trick," he said. "Dr. Winston seems to know what he's doing."

"I don't know if I trust him," she said peevishly. "He's too young. A young doctor just doesn't have the experience."

She watched him as he raised the paper. It slanted across his face, leaving his eyes exposed. Now was the time, she thought. Before he had a chance to think. "Arthur?" she said.

"Yes, dear?"

"Who is Jessica?"

His eyebrows raised a fraction. He lowered the paper, his face blank and composed. "Who?"

"Jessica," she repeated.

He frowned, concentrating. "I don't believe I know any Jessica. Why? Should I?"

"I was just wondering, Arthur. You said her name in your sleep last night."

He laughed and set down the paper. "That's incredible," he said. "I swear to you, I've never known a Jessica in my life. I can't figure out why on earth I'd mention the name in my sleep." He grinned at her. "Maybe I'm the one who should see Dr. Winston."

She didn't answer him and he went back to his paper. You're very good, she thought bitterly. How many men can tell a lie so calmly? But then you've had so much practice over the past eight years. She felt like crying again so she went into the living room and smoked another cigarette

A few minutes later Arthur came in with his topcoat and briefcase.

"Why are you leaving so early?" she asked.

"Paul and I have to check a few things," he said. "May as well get a head start." His lips brushed her cheek. "Perhaps we'll drop in on the Gordons tonight. They wanted us to come over for weeks."

She turned and looked through the window. "It depends. We'll see how I'm feeling."

"Fine." He went to the door. "Try to get a little sun, Lenore. I'll have the gardener put out the lounge. It'll be good for you."

She nodded vaguely and he closed the door. She watched him walk down the flagged path and across the lawn to the gardener's cottage. The new gardener would be told to put out the lounge, but he would deliberately forget; he was almost as lazy as the maid. Why did the servants continually try to spite her? Why did they go out of their way to upset her when they knew she wasn't well?

The blue Cadillac backed down the drive and into the street. On the way, Arthur caught sight of her at the window and waved, smiling. She didn't bother to wave back. The car moved slowly down the block until she could no longer see it.

Mrs. Dunning turned from the window. It was only nine-thirty in the morning and she was practically out of cigarettes. Her head felt uncomfortable and there was a pain in the small of her back. She dropped into a chair.

A probing voice persisted in asking her questions. Who is Jessica? Is she pretty? Is she young and healthy? Why did he run away to work when you mentioned her name?

Mrs. Dunning had a certain urge to enter the bedroom. She knew she mustn't, that it was just to torture herself, but she had to go.

She looked at her face in the mirror, looked at it searchingly in the strong sunlight. There was gray showing in her hair and pouches under her eyes. Thirty-nine years old and the mirror said fifty. No wonder he was tired of her and taking up with other women. But her anger caught up with the pity. He had no right to leave her alone. She might be growing old, but that was no reason for him to find himself a Jessica.

Mrs. Dunning lit her last cigarette and sat down on the bed. He knows I won't give him a divorce, she thought. I wouldn't doubt it if he was thinking of killing me. The notion jarred her, sent her heart hammering. No, he wouldn't try anything like that. He didn't have the nerve.

She got up and closed the bedroom door. The maid was starting to vacuum the downstairs hallway and the machine made a high, buzzing sound through the house. Kill me! The thought left her cold and dizzy. Suppose he had planned something with Dr. Winston, paid him money to give her a bottle of poisoned pills. No, it was impossible. She had been taking the pills for a week now and nothing had happened to her. But perhaps it was slow-action poison, a drug that took weeks or even months. The pain shot through her back. Oh God, she moaned, maybe it was the pills. But the pain soon subsided and she lay back on the bed, shaking. She was dizzy again, and very sleepy.

The telephone rang. It sat on the table next to the bed and the sound jerked her upward. She waited for the maid to answer it downstairs.

"Mrs. Dunning?" The maid's voice drifted from the floor below. "Your husband's on the phone, Mrs. Dunning. Shall I tell him you're resting?"

"No," she called. "I'll take it." She lifted the receiver. "Hello, Arthur?"

"How are you feeling?" he said.

Why is he calling? she wondered. He never calls in the morning. "Not – not very well," she said.

"What's wrong?" He sounded genuinely concerned.

"I'm dizzy. And I have a headache."

"Call the doctor. He can send something over."

"No, I'll be all right," she said. "It's really not anything."

"Well, listen. I have some bad news."

She was instantly on her guard. "What is it?"

"I have to take a trip tonight. Mexico City. Something came up and Paul thinks I should get down there as soon as possible."

Now he had finally gone too far. "Arthur," she said, "you never go to Mexico until the fall. Not once in eight years."

"I know, but this is urgent. One of our dealers wants to go with a competitor. He's a good man; we don't want to lose him."

"Let Paul go," she said. "He can handle it."

"I don't think so. I know the guy, so it has to be me. It won't take long. I'll be back tomorrow night. I won't even take clothes with me."

"I don't like it, Arthur," she said. "I'll be all alone here."

"Lenore, for heaven's sake," he said. "You've been alone before. The maid's there."

"I don't like it," she repeated.

"Honey, don't be childish. The doors have locks and chains. There hasn't been a robbery in the neighborhood for years. Can't you sit up with a glass of milk and watch television?"

"Arthur, I —"

He interrupted her. "Only a day, Lenore. Is that a lifetime?"

"No, but —"

"So I'll see you soon. I'll call you tonight from the airport."

"All right," she said, weak and knowing there was nothing she could say to dissuade him.

"Oh, Lenore," he said, "I remembered that name. Jessica."

She stiffened, gripping the phone tighter.

"The name I said in my sleep. It was the plane I flew in the war. The B-17; we called it 'Jessica' for some reason. Probably someone's wife or girl, I don't remember. Satisfied?"

"Yes," she said, almost whispering.

"I guess I was reliving a bombing mission. Up there with the guys again. Good old Jessica, she really held up." There was a pause. "Well, I have to go. Lock the doors tight and you'll be fine. Do your hair. The time'll fly. Okay? Bye, dear."

The connection clicked gently. She could imagine him hanging up, the shadow of a smile on his face. He was probably dialing again, Jessica's number.

Mrs. Dunning sat down on the bed. What a ridiculous story. His B-17 in the war! It was getting serious when he didn't even take the time to concoct a believable lie.

She went downstairs and tried to read a magazine, but she was too nervous. She told the maid not to prepare lunch and went into the study. The window was wide open and the sun patterned the carpet with thick, bright bands. Mrs. Dunning massaged her temples and then closed the window, drawing the heavy curtains. The room was half-dark. She sat down in Arthur's leather chair and leaned back, trying to relax.

Where had he been stationed during the war? She hadn't known him then, but he had often mentioned his base. It was in England. That was it! The Hambledon Air Force Base in England. She wondered if the airfield was still there, if they kept track of the old bomber planes. They must have some sort of record.

She switched on the desk lamp and paged through the telephone directory. Under "United States Dept. of Air Force" was a long listing of numbers. She picked one that looked suitable and then dialed.

"Yes, sir?" said a pleasant voice.

"I would like some information," she said. "My husband was with the Air Force during the Second World War, and I was wondering if there was some way I might find out the name of his plane."

"The name of his plane? I don't understand, ma'am."

Her mind went blank for a moment. Then she said lightly, "Well, it's his birthday. I bought him a silver lighter, the kind he used when he was in the service. I thought it might be nice if I had the name of his old plane engraved on it."

"It's probably on file somewhere, ma'am. Those planes are pretty much obsolete by now, but they'd have a listing. You could try Washington. Or else contact your husband's old base."

"But it's in England," she said. "It would take weeks and weeks to find out."

"I'm sorry, ma'am. That'd be the best way. Unless – say, if you want to find out the name of the plane, why don't you just ask your husband?"

She let the phone drop on its cradle. Idiotic red tape! The call had not helped her at all. And there was no way to contact the crew. She didn't even know them, and Arthur had once told her they were scattered all over the country.

In the late afternoon she retired to the bedroom and shut out the sunlight. She lay down in a square world of darkness, letting a sleeping pill numb her mind. She slept deeply, not remembering a thing from the time her head hit the pillow. But it seemed that only minutes later something was jabbing her. She sat up and realized that the phone was ringing. There was night along the edge of the curtains.

Arthur was calling from the airport. He sounded cheerful and said he'd see her the next evening. She was still affected by the sleeping pill, and she mumbled something unintelligible. He didn't seem to notice. She hung up and fell back on the bed, pulling the blanket over her.

When she opened her eyes late the following morning she was aware of a great, hollow silence in the house. Birds sang in the trees, and she could hear the gardener clipping hedges beyond the lawn.

She got up and pulled on her dressing gown. Then, quite suddenly, she understood why the house was so quiet. It was Thursday, the maid's day off. She would be alone for hours, no one to talk to, no one to protect her. How in heaven's name could Arthur have been so cruel?

Mrs. Dunning wandered through the rooms. The air was warm and close, the whole house pulsed with heat. She went to the study and dialed her husband's office. A woman answered, "Cross and Dunning."

Mrs. Dunning tensed. She didn't recognize the voice. Had Arthur hired a new secretary?

"Hello," she said. "Who is this speaking?"

"Mr. Dunning's secretary," the young voice answered.

"This is Mrs. Dunning. What is your name, young lady?"

"Carolyn. Carolyn Sharpless." The voice sounded puzzled.

Was she lying? Had Arthur put her up to this, told her to use another name? Perhaps Paul was in on it, too.

"I'd like to speak with Mr. Cross," she said.

"Just a moment."

There was a delay, then a slight click. "Lenore!" boomed Paul's hearty voice. "How are you feeling?"

"A little better, thank you, Paul. How are you?"

"Great. Had a checkup last week. Doctor says I've got the system of a man of thirty."

"Paul," she said cautiously, "is my husband there?"

"Arthur? Didn't he tell you? He had to fly down to Mexico City last night."

"Oh, yes, yes, of course he did." He must think I've lost my mind, she thought. Or else he knows I'm checking and he's on his guard. "Paul, was it such an urgent situation that he had to go away so suddenly?"

"I'm afraid it was, Lenore. Involves a lot of money."

"But couldn't you have gone? Instead of Arthur, I mean."

He hesitated. "Well…yes. But Arthur knows the man down there. We thought it best for him to handle it alone."

"Did he talk you into thinking that?" she said sharply.

"Why no, Lenore. We both came to the same conclusion. Is something wrong? You sound worried."

"No, Paul. Nothing's wrong. Actually, I called to ask you about something else."

"What's that?"

"I know Arthur doesn't talk very much about his war experience, but has he ever mentioned the name of his old plane to you?"

"What plane?" he said, confused.

"The B-17 he flew during the war. Did he ever tell you what they called it?"

"No. I don't think so. Why?"

"Just – just something I wanted to know. Nothing important. Thank you, Paul."

She replaced the receiver, her head spinning. If only she had a cigarette she could think. The ashtray was filled with crushed stubs, and she picked out one of the longer ones. As she lit it, her hand shook.

Why had he gone to Mexico City? There could only be one reason – an alibi. He was going as far away as possible to make it look good; he'd get involved in business and surround himself with witnesses. He had probably hired someone he could trust to do the job, a professional murderer, an expert. She had read about them in the papers. They worked quietly and skillfully, observing their victims, then moving in when the time was right.

Her hand closed around the phone. She could still call the police. But they wouldn't believe her; they'd laugh. Jessica? Jessica who? You need more proof than that, lady. But he's lying. That wasn't the name of his plane. Really? Prove it.

She went to the window and threw open the curtains on the harsh sun. Now she wanted light, as much as possible. The police were the answer, of course, but she needed evidence, something that would convince them. She closed her eyes, straining to think. How could she discover the name of the plane? Records, files? No, it would take too long.

Suddenly she smiled. His war souvenirs! Of course. He kept them in the attic. And now that she thought of it there was a picture among them, a photograph of the plane and the crew. If the name of the plane was in the picture…

She ran upstairs, almost tripping on the folds of her robe. She unlocked the door in the hallway and went up a narrow, dusty flight of steps. The attic was thick with heat and cobwebs, cooking under the wooden rafters. She pushed aside a wicker chair and some iron garden furniture. Crates and cardboard boxes were stacked against the wall. She overturned some of them, moved a few away, and finally found the large carton marked AIR FORCE in crayon.

Mrs. Dunning ripped it open and poured the contents on the floor. There were a few khaki hats, some medals and copies of orders, a packet of snapshots, and a long. cardboard tube. She picked up the tube and groped inside, sliding out a rolled photograph. The picture was yellowing slightly, but when she unrolled it the faces of the crew, standing by the silver bomber, were still distinct. And there was a name stenciled below the cockpit in heavy black paint, right over the head of Captain Arthur Dunning. The name was JESSICA.

For the first time in two days, Mrs. Dunning broke down and cried. She knelt on the floor of the attic, her head bent. What a fool she had been.

She left the things on the floor and went downstairs. In the sunny bathroom she washed her face and changed into a fresh dress. She combed her hair and put on lipstick. She was a foolish woman, a foolish neurotic woman. She had been jealous and full of self-pity, her imagination had gotten out of hand. All of that would have to change. She decided that when Arthur returned home she'd make him buy her a little car. I'll have my freedom again, she thought. I'll get out to see my old friends.

She felt enormously hungry, and she went to the kitchen to make herself something to eat. Then she went back to the attic to put the souvenirs away. There was no sense leaving a mess for the maid to straighten out.

She looked at the photograph again, smiling at Arthur's youthful face. Then she felt a sudden chill. The man standing next to her husband looked very familiar. It was almost as if she had seen him recently.

But that was impossible. Her imagination was playing tricks. Unless…She brought a hand up to her mouth. Unless she had been right all along! That would explain why he mentioned the Jessica in his sleep. The plane was on his mind, the plane and his old crew member whom he had hired to –

"Mrs. Dunning?"

Someone was speaking softly from the doorway behind her. She turned, sucking in her breath, and saw the face of the man in the photograph.

The new gardener stepped toward her. There was a large, shining pair of shears in his gloved hand.

NO NAME, ADDRESS, IDENTITY

There was a jolt, a tremendous and brutal impact, and for a fraction of a second the young man's senses turned topsy-turvy. The sun suddenly seemed to be below him and the sky, spinning over his head, became asphalt. He plunged into the street, rolled and landed with his cheek against the rough edge of the curb.

"Somebody help that man!" screamed a woman.

"I saw it!" cried another voice. "Hit and run! Get the license number!"

He became dimly aware that he was surrounded by people. The sky had righted itself and a ring of concerned faces hung over his head. Painfully, he pushed himself to his knees.

"Better not move, pal." This from a truck driver type in a leather windbreaker. "They're gettin' a cop now. He'll call an ambulance."

"No," he said. "No, I'm – I'm all right." He started getting unsteadily to his feet.

"I saw it all," said a woman proudly. "You were crossing the street and car hit a puddle of water. Skidded right into you. Then took off like I don't know what."

"Sure you're okay?" The truck driver again.

"I don't think it's wise to move," added an elderly woman in a mink coat. "You might have broken something."

"Just – knocked the wind out of me," the young man said, on his feet now. "I'm fine," he added, forcing a smile.

They stood there watching him until someone handed him his hat. "Well… thanks," he said awkwardly. "Now if you'll…excuse me. I have an appointment."

They moved back, opening a corridor so that he could pass. He walked through them, testing every step, but there was no sharp signal of discomfort to indicate a fracture or even a strain. His head was bruised and his hand was cut, but that was all.

When he was a few blocks away he paused to light a cigarette. I must lead a charmed life, he thought. Knocked down by some maniac and no damage done. I could have been killed. He patted himself again, in wonderment. Then he decided he'd better hurry; he had to keep his appointment.

What appointment?

It suddenly occurred to him that he didn't know who he was, hadn't the faintest idea.

The young man stopped, quelling a momentary surge of panic. Of course he knew who he was. A name just doesn't drop out of the mind. He was…he was…

It would come to him. He was just a little rattled by the accident. Shock, maybe. A temporary lapse of memory. He snapped his cigarette away and started walking again, concentrating. But nothing came. He couldn't even decide if he had been on this street or in this city before. He paused in front of a shop window and studied his reflection. Well, it was an average face, a face he must have seen every day for close to thirty-five years. But it was totally unfamiliar.

This is ridiculous, he thought. Something you read in the newspapers. He had been crossing the street, minding his own business, and by some blunder of fate a skidding car had snatched away his powers of recollection. Amnesia. Like something on the Late Late Show. He didn't even know what he did for a living. A lawyer? A businessman? And where did he live? Was he rich or poor, married or single?

His wallet! There'd be identification in his wallet. The young man plunged his hands into his pockets, but there was nothing except a key ring, cigarettes, and some change. He patted his back pocket. Nothing. Just a handkerchief.

But that was impossible. Surely, whoever he was, he carried a wallet. Unless…He looked back over his shoulder. Unless he had dropped it during the confusion of the accident. He'd better go back and try to find it.

He started to retrace his steps, but before he had gone a block he realized he was lost. Had he made a right turn or a left? Was it down this street or two blocks away? There were no landmarks to guide him; nothing looked familiar, yet nothing looked strange. He finally stopped, helpless, and began another frantic search of his clothing.

Jacket pockets, nothing. Trouser pockets, nothing. Inside jacket pocket…His groping fingers touched something and, eagerly, he pulled it out. Then, stunned, he stared at what he held in his hand. It was a stiff, new thousand-dollar bill, and wrapped around it was a sheet of notepaper. There was writing on the paper and he unfolded it.

> Dr. Ralph Mannix
> Medical Building
> 23 West 86th

Mannix, Mannix. He felt no response to the name; no note of memory was struck. But it was the only clue he had. He hurried to the corner and looked up at the street sign. West 79th. He was seven blocks away. He stuffed the bill back into his pocket and started walking, faster and faster, until he was actually running. People glanced at him, wondering at his haste, but he didn't care.

When he came into the waiting room, the receptionist was busy typing. She finished a sentence, threw the carriage, and swiveled to meet him. "May I help –" she began, then stopped.

The young man stood just inside the doorway, out of breath. The look on her face made him conscious of his torn suit and bruised forehead.

She cleared her throat. "May I help you?"

"Is Doctor Mannix in?" he said.

"Yes, but he's leaving for the day. Do you have an appointment?"

He paused. "I…don't know."

"I beg your pardon?"

"Look, just buzz him. It's important."

"I'm sorry, but I'll have to have your name."

"Lady, if I knew my name I wouldn't be here."

He watched her study him for a moment. Then, apparently sensing the urgency of his manner, she picked up the phone and rang the inner office. "A gentleman is here to see you, Doctor."

A few seconds later a door opened and Doctor Mannix looked out. He was an older man, with hair gone gray at the temples and pink, freckled hands. His eyes, behind the sharp circles of his glasses, were tranquil. In a pleasant voice he said, "Yes?"

The young man crossed the room quickly. "Doctor Mannix?"

"That's right."

"Doctor, do you – do you know who I am?" Having said it, he felt like a fool. "I mean, have you ever met me before?"

The doctor seemed puzzled. "No, I don't believe so. Why?"

"Are you sure?"

"Quite sure. And that's a nasty cut on your head. I'd better have a look at it."

The young man touched his temple and his hand came away with a trace of red.

"It's opened up and needs attention. Come inside." Mannix stepped into the other room and indicated a leather chair near a window. "Sit down and I'll be right with you." He disappeared into an alcove, still talking. "My nurse just left a few minutes ago. We were closing up shop for the day."

The young man dropped into the chair and massaged his eyes. He looked from the framed diplomas on the wall to the gathering darkness in the sky outside the window. He was depressed and tired, but he was afraid to allow himself to doze. The whole incident might take place again in some corner of his mind – the jolt, the feeling of falling through space, and then the hard edge of the curb against his cheek.

Mannix returned with a bottle of alcohol and a wad of cotton. "This will sting, but it'll fix you up." He bent down and swabbed the wound, adjusting his glasses and examining it critically. "No stitching necessary. You're lucky it wasn't deeper." He went to a metal table, pulled out a drawer, and came up with a roll of bandages. "I'd rather let the air at it, but it's not very pretty to look at. So –" With sure, strong motions he pressed the dressing over the cut and stepped back. "There. Good as new."

The young man ran a tentative finger along the bandage. "I guess I really got knocked around," he said. "That's why it happened."

"Why what happened?"

The young man hesitated for a moment, then he sighed. "I

may as well tell you," he said. "I can't remember who I am."

Mannix studied him, then capped the bottle of alcohol and set it on the metal table. He moved behind his desk and sat down, elbows on the blotter, his fingers laced. He didn't say anything.

"Look, I know this sounds crazy, but about an hour ago I was crossing the street and a car smashed into me." The young man dug into his pocket for a cigarette. "Some damn fool was driving, I guess. He skidded, clipped me, and then took off like a rocket. Didn't even stop to see if I was hurt."

"Anyone get the license number?"

"No. There was too much excitement. I was hit and the next thing I knew there was a crowd around me. Somebody was going for an ambulance and everybody was yelling not to touch me. I felt all right, though – a little cut up, but no bones broken." The young man lit the cigarette and exhaled smoke. His throat was dry. "Anyway, I got to my feet and told them I wasn't hurt. I wanted to get out of there. Crowds make me nervous."

The door opened and the receptionist looked in. "I'm leaving now, Doctor. Unless you need me."

"No. I'll see you in the morning, Miss Sherman." She closed the door softly and Mannix picked up a letter opener from his desk. He toyed with it absently, balancing it between his fingers. "Were you aware of striking your head with any force?" he asked.

It happened so fast I didn't have a chance to notice. One minute I was crossing the street, the next I felt this thing smash into me."

"What happened then?"

The young man explained about his walk and his sudden feeling of panic when he realized he couldn't remember his name. The doctor listened carefully, then began to nod. "Temporary amnesia," he said.

"Are you positive?"

"Just about. Temporary amnesia is produced by shock or a sharp blow." He got up and took the young man's wrist. He glanced at his watch as he continued to hold the wrist. "Your pulse is normal. Any headache, dizziness, or nausea?"

"No, nothing like that."

"You might have a slight concussion. It's difficult to tell without an X-ray and a complete examination." The doctor looked at him. "Why did you come to me, by the way?"

"That's the funny part. When I searched my pockets all I found was a thousand-dollar bill. And wrapped around it was a piece of paper with your name and address on it."

The doctor was surprised. "My name?"

"That's right. At first I thought I might be you, I mean that I might be Doctor Mannix. And I figured if I wasn't, you'd probably know who I was. Why else would I have your name in my pocket? So I came over here."

"This is most peculiar. I'm sure I've never seen you before. Perhaps a patient of mine gave you the name and address."

The young man stubbed his cigarette into an ashtray. "The question is, what do I do now?"

Mannix thought for a moment. "I suppose you should go to the police. Tell them what happened and have them publish your photograph in the paper. If you have any relatives in this town, they'll see it and come for you." He reached for the phone. "I'll call and have them send a car."

"No." The young man held up his hand. He was annoyed. "Look, I don't want to make a thing out of this. All I want is to remember my name. I thought you could help me."

"The best way is for me to call the —"

The young man stood up, slapping his fist irritably against his palm. "This is ridiculous. I keep thinking I'm dreaming. A thousand-dollar bill and no name." He wheeled on the doctor. "Can it go away? I mean, can I get my memory back?"

"Sometimes the lapse lasts only a few hours. Once in a while something makes a connection and the mind returns to normal. But it's difficult to say. The only sure way is treatment. If you'll just let me —"

The young man stared at a framed photograph on the desk. "Who's that?" he asked.

Puzzled, Mannix glanced at the picture. "My wife. Why?"

"I don't know. Maybe — I wonder if I have a wife."

"If you do, she's probably worried. Now listen to me. Let me call the police and go down there with you. They have doctors.

We can give you a thorough examination. Besides, they may have had inquiries."

The young man wasn't paying attention. He went over to the window and looked out. "This is the weirdest thing," he said. "The weirdest thing." He turned apologetically. "Look, I'm sorry I bothered you. I guess you want to go home."

Before Mannix could protest, the young man made an abrupt motion of farewell and headed for the door. "I'll work this out," he called back over his shoulder. "Don't worry."

"But listen –"

"I'll be fine." He walked hurriedly through the empty waiting room and out into the empty corridor, relieved to be alone. He had been nervous in the doctor's office; it was almost as bad as when he was lying on his back an hour ago with a ring of curious faces hanging over him. Besides, his head was beginning to throb.

He pressed the elevator button and concentrated on the floor indicator as it traveled in a slow arc. For some reason the photograph of the doctor's wife floated before his eyes, terribly annoying in its familiarity.

And then, quite suddenly, he remembered who he was.

The elevator doors slid open, then closed, but he remained where he was, marveling at the surge of recollection that filled his brain. Everything had come back to him, he was himself again, and he began to laugh as he about-faced and walked towards the doctor's office.

Mannix was just turning out the lights when he came in. "Doctor, this is really amazing, but it hit me while I was waiting for the elevator. It happened all of a sudden, like a flash."

"You mean your memory came back?"

"Everything." The young man was elated. "I even know where the thousand bucks came from."`

"Really?"

"Your wife gave it to me."

"My wife?" The doctor's eyes widened behind his glasses.

"Sure," said the young man, reaching for the long, metal letter opener on the desk. He smiled. "That's what she paid me to kill you."

THE END OF AN ERA

It was an absolute nuisance, something to be endured like a session in the dentist's chair. Mr. Grubb found himself wishing that he could close his ears with invisible plugs. They were talking about him, paying false tribute to his fifteen years with the firm, and the one thing he didn't want to do was listen. But he was forced to smile and nod, trying to look shy and grateful at the same time. He squirmed in his seat, consoling himself with the knowledge that it couldn't last much longer. And within forty-eight hours – he was delighted by the irony – they'd all see this little gathering in a different light.

"Those mornings by the water cooler," Miss Lemmon was saying. "Why, I'd just peek over at Mr. Grubb behind his desk and I'd say to myself, 'There's the man for me.' But he never even gave me a tumble. Did you, Miles?"

There was laughter. Why shouldn't they laugh, he reflected; he was old enough to be her grandfather. The little flirt knew he was married, too, but that didn't stop her, she had to make a conquest of every man in the office, young or old, and he was no exception.

While they all laughed, he made himself smile the idiot grin of the good sport. Then Miss Lemmon sat down and there was a hush in the room as Mr. Dougherty got ponderously to his feet. Well, here come the platitudes, thought Mr. Grubb. The fifteen years of unswerving service to the firm, the feeling of personal loss at this particular retirement. Mr. Grubb permitted himself a small smile. There'd be loss, all right, and much more personal than Dougherty expected. He settled back as his employer began to speak, wondering if they'd have the staggering effrontery to give him a wristwatch.

"I'll be brief," Mr. Dougherty was saying, gazing out over his staff like a benevolent shepherd. "The end of an era is not a time for chatter, it's a time for thought. And when Miles Grubb leaves this office today it *will* be the end of an era, a moment for all of us here at Cumberland, Inc. to take stock of ourselves and our company."

Having promised to be brief, he launched into a lengthy oration. Mr. Grubb, bored, cast his eye around the office. His co-workers were listening with the proper look of reverence; they sat behind their desks, completely absorbed, their thoughts no doubt winging to the day of their own retirement. He grunted under his breath. They were all such fools; their white collars were choking them and they didn't even know it. Well, it wasn't for him. He had intelligence and ambition; he intended to spend the last years of his life in unfettered luxury. And Mr. Dougherty, poor, bumbling Mr. Dougherty, would provide the means.

The speech ran down of its own sheer weight and Mr. Grubb was asked to stand. "Miles," said his employer, "there's very little we can do to show our appreciation on this, your last day here at Cumberland." He held up a wrapped package. "But we hope this small gift will stand as a token of our esteem."

There was applause. Mr. Grubb crossed the office, past the two buckets of iced champagne near the filing cabinets, past the desk where he had labored for fifteen years, and with just the right show of bashfulness he took the package from Dougherty's pink hands. "I'd like to thank –" he began.

"Open it," shouted Rudy Schmidt, the billing clerk.

"Yes, Miles, let's see," said Miss Lemmon.

Dutifully, he peeled away the layers of paper and opened the box. Inside was a matching lighter and ashtray set. A small card read: "To Miles from the Gang at the Office." He winced. "This is – this is very nice," he said. "Thank you."

Then everyone was standing around clapping him on the shoulder. With twin pops the champagne corks were pulled and someone brought glasses from Mr. Dougherty's private office. A toast was proposed, then another. Mr. Grubb was compelled to drink to Miss Lemmon, to Cumberland, Inc., to the free enterprise system. It struck him that it would never do to get drunk; there was much to accomplish before the day was over. Fortunately, the big wall clock was inching toward six and a few people were already going for their coats.

Finally it was over. Mr. Dougherty drove off in his limousine and the warehouse men came from the back to punch out. Mr. Grubb stuffed his few belongings in his overcoat pockets, tucked the gift under his arm, and headed for the door. He was stopped by Alvin Griggle, the assistant comptroller.

"Gotta take you out and buy you a drink," said Alvin.

"Thanks, but I have to get home for dinner. The wife's expecting me."

Alvin's face drooped, then brightened. "Yeah, guess so," he said. "But I'll miss you, buddy. You don't know how lucky you are to be leaving this place." He shook his head. "I've been here ten years myself. And what does it get me? A hundred twenty-five, less deductions. It isn't worth it, Miles. Look at you. Fifteen years. And you wind up with a lighter and a glass of champagne."

Mr. Grubb was touched. The man seemed on the verge of tears. "I'll get by, Alvin," he said. Then he smiled. "I'll get by very well."

He left the office and went into a hotel across the street to phone his wife, telling her he'd be late for dinner. Then he bought a paper and read the news until seven-thirty. When it was dark outside he left the hotel and crossed the windy pavements to a bus terminal. There, in one of the wall lockers, he found the suitcase he had left there that morning. Everything was fine, he told himself. Just fine.

It was almost eight o'clock when he let himself into the Cumberland office. The place was dark but he didn't need a flashlight; after fifteen years he could have moved around the desks and partitions blindfolded. He crossed to Mr. Dougherty's office, went inside, and put down his suitcase, orienting himself. The safe was concealed by paneling to the left of the door. Mr. Grubb chuckled. Its location was an open secret to everyone in the office.

He touched a hidden device to slide the panel aside, remembering quite clearly the day the safe had been delivered. Mr. Dougherty had beamed proudly, instructing the workmen in the mechanics of its installation. Mr. Grubb had come into the office to discuss an accounting error and had noticed, completely by accident, a slip of paper on his employer's desk. It contained, in neat, ballpoint lettering, the combination of the safe. Grubb remembered those numerals. They had stayed in a corner of his brain for the past two years, always available and ready for use.

Now, with his fingers turning the dial, he felt a quiet touch of triumph. First the money, then the plane ticket resting in a drawer at home, and finally the flight to Hawaii, to Brazil, to some lush spot beyond extradition where he could sit and watch a hundred tropical suns come in and out with the tide.

All thanks for Mr. Dougherty and his habit of keeping large amounts of cash on hand. Carefully, quietly, Mr. Grubb opened the safe and lit a match. Ranged on the shelves before his eyes were neat stacks of currency in bank wrappers. He wouldn't even have to count them; each packet had its total value stamped on the wrapper. Mr. Grubb brought his suitcase to the mouth of the safe and began removing money. It was, he reflected, the last transaction he would ever perform for Cumberland, Inc.

The first thing his wife said when he came into the house was, "How was your party, dear?"

He examined her critically and decided he wouldn't miss her at all. In the beginning, when he was formulating his plan, he had hesitated for weeks over whether or not to take her with him. But now, looking at the wrinkled face, the gray hair and the vacant eyes, he was positive he had made the right choice. She didn't even ask him why he was carrying his suitcase; he had an excuse ready and waiting, but apparently all she could think of was the party.

"Very pleasant," he said. "They gave me a lighter and matching ashtrays."

"Oh, how lovely. Where are they?"

He suddenly remembered he had put them in the suitcase. "I have them," he said. "I'll show them to you later. Now I think I'd better wash up."

"Of course, dear."

She bustled into the kitchen and he went upstairs. In their bedroom he opened the suitcase and set the office gift on the dresser. Then he looked at the money for a long moment, trying to picture what would happen on Monday morning. Dougherty would be livid. Probably wouldn't even believe it at first. Not Miles Grubb.

How could he do such a thing? And after fifteen years with the firm.

He began loading a few essentials into the suitcase. He'd buy the rest, clothes and everything, when he reached his destination. Then he took the plane ticket from his drawer, went to the hall extension phone, and dialed the airline. Flight 106 would be leaving for Hawaii on schedule? Eleven o'clock? Thank you very much. He closed the suitcase and went down to dinner.

The meal was uneventful. His wife chattered aimlessly and he only half listened while he ate. She was telling him that they could now enjoy the benefits of leisure. "You'll have all this time on your hands," she said. "So I was thinking...Dear? Did you hear me?"

"Yes. You were thinking..."

"And I thought it might be nice if we took a drive across the country. You've always wanted to travel and we could stop by Cleveland and see my sister." The idea seemed to excite her. "We don't have to push it or anything. Just a slow, pleasant drive. After all, we're getting older, and we might not have the chance unless we do it soon."

She might be getting older, thought Mr. Grubb, but he felt ageless. For a moment he was sorry for her; she'd live out the remainder of her days in this house, never once tasting, touching, seeing, and death would come as a favor. He wondered how she'd feel when she found out he had betrayed her. Would she be angry, would she cry, would she condemn or defend him? No, she'd probably accept the whole thing with her usual passivity. Well, that was her problem, not his. She'd vanish from his memory the moment he got on the plane.

After dinner she went into the kitchen to do the dishes. Mr. Grubb silently climbed to the bedroom, slipped the ticket into his breast pocket, and lifted the suitcase. He glanced around for the last time and was pleased to find that no chords were struck; there wasn't even a slight twinge of nostalgia. Smiling, he went downstairs and left the suitcase by the door.

"I'm going to take a drive," he said. "Get some fresh air."

"All right, dear. Bring back the paper when you come, will you?"

"Of course."

He bent to kiss the back of her neck. Then he left her there, arms plunged in soapy water, gray hair wispy in the steam. No, he decided, he wouldn't miss her at all.

Everything went smoothly at the airport. He left his car in the parking area with the keys in the ignition. It was a small gesture of kindness – now they wouldn't have to tow it away. Inside the terminal building he dropped his suitcase on the scales at the check-in counter and it was comfortably underweight. Well, money wasn't heavy, he reflected, at least not in the physical sense. He bought a few magazines and a box of cough drops, then browsed until loudspeakers began announcing his flight.

Settled on the plane, his seat belt fastened and his magazines on his lap, Mr. Grubb sighed a sigh of contentment. He was safe; there hadn't been a single hitch in plans. Within a few minutes the engines would roar, they would taxi down the runway, and then, lifting, lifting, he'd be carried toward Hawaii and gilt-edged anonymity. He waited, his mind pleasantly occupied with thoughts of the things he would buy, for the propellers to grind into life.

And the stewardess' voice was speaking over the PA system. "Ladies and gentlemen, due to mechanical difficulties we'll be unable to take off on schedule. We'd appreciate it if you'd leave by the rear door and go to the main waiting room until further notice."

There was a discontented murmur from the other passengers. Mr. Grubb frowned. Always some idiotic fly in the ointment. And he had just been congratulating himself on how smoothly thing were going. Well, they'd get it straightened out, whatever it was. He unfastened his seatbelt and joined the others inching down the aisle.

As soon as he reached the waiting room he crossed to the check-in counter. "How long will 106 be delayed?" he asked.

"We don't know, sir," said the young man smoothly. "An hour, maybe more."

"What's the problem?"

"Just a few mechanical difficulties. Nothing serious."

Mr. Grubb found a chair and tried to read his magazine, but his eye was constantly drawn to the check-in counter. It seemed to be the meeting spot of a group of officials; they were talking animatedly among themselves, then one would hurry off and someone else would join the circle. He got up and moved closer to them, trying to overhear, but their voices were pitched too low. Finally, deciding it had nothing to do with his flight, he started back to his seat.

And then he saw the police officers, four of them come into the building and move toward the desk. There was a hurried conference and they headed through double doors to the landing field.

He resisted a momentary impulse to run. But they couldn't be here after him. It was impossible. He made himself relax by an effort of will. No one would enter the Cumberland office until Monday morning. Then and only then would be the police be interested in his whereabouts.

Mr. Grubb paged through his magazine as time stretched on. His flight had been delayed a half hour now and he was growing nervous. The cluster at the check-in counter had dispersed and a new man – he seemed to be younger than the other – possibly new on the job – was weighing in luggage. Mr. Grubb watched him for a moment. These airline people never tell you anything, he thought, but this fellow had the look of inexperience about him. Perhaps he could be bullied into parting with some information. Mr. Grubb stood and approached the counter.

"Look," he said in an angry voice, "we've been waiting here for thirty-five minutes. What's happening with 106 to Hawaii?"

"Just some minor diff –"

"I don't believe it," he snapped. "There's something else. Now do you tell me what it is or do I go to your superior?"

"Really, sir –"

"Don't 'really, sir' me! There were four police officers here a while ago. Why? What's going on?"

He continued to raise his voice and the young man looked uncomfortable.

"Well – if I tell you, sir, will you promise you won't tell the other passengers?"

"I promise."

The young man hesitated for a moment, then said, "We got a

crank call. You know, it happens every one in a while. Something about a bomb on the plane."

"A bomb?"

"No truth to it, of course. But we have to check. As soon as they've finished you'll be taking off."

Mr. Grubb felt immensely relieved. Just a silly anonymous phone call. Some crank who hated the world. It had nothing to do with him at all. "I appreciate your telling me," he said, "and I'll keep quiet about it. How much longer will it take them?"

"Another ten, fifteen minutes, I guess. They have to search the luggage."

Mr. Grubb stared at him. "Search the luggage?"

"Yes, sir. Just a normal precaution."

Mr. Grubb felt his heart pumping abnormally. He reeled away from the desk, just in time to see a police officer come through the double doors and start toward him.

The man held his suitcase in his hand.

"He wants you to call your family lawyer and come down to police headquarters right away," said the voice on the telephone.

"But – I don't understand," said Mrs. Grubb.

"Neither do we, lady. All we know is that he had a fortune in that suitcase of his."

Mrs. Grubb had difficulty speaking.

"We're at the airport," said the policeman. "We're leaving now and we'll be at the station house in twenty minutes."

"Is he – under arrest?"

"Yes, ma'am."

"Then tell him – tell him I'll call Bill Moore and we'll both be down there right away. Tell him everything will be all right."

The police officer hung up and Mrs. Grubb stood looking at the telephone for a long time. Then she dialed the airline terminal. When someone answered the phone she said, "I called you before, about that bomb on flight 106."

"Who is this?" said the voice sharply.

"Never mind. I just wanted to say there isn't any bomb. You can leave now, if you want to."

"If you'd give me your name –"

"Tell them down there it was all a joke. That's all it was. Just a joke."

She hung up, smiled, and began to dial the family lawyer.

TOP-FLIGHT AQUARIUM

Jimmy stood in the lobby of the Hotel Pacific, looking down at the steady stream of cars heading west on Wilshire Boulevard. Every so often a big convertible or a brisk sports model would race by, the driver tanned and comfortably bored behind the wheel. It was after dinner and dark, with a breeze, sharp and salty, from the ocean.

Jimmy watched the silent glide of cars wistfully. That's pretty nice living, he thought. Have yourself a lobster in one of those open-air restaurants that lean over the sea, and then take a blanket and lie on the sand with your wife and kids. Real nice, with the wind coming in off the water and all the money in the world.

He moved away from the glass doors and glanced around the empty lobby. It was only nine o'clock but the hotel seemed hushed and deserted. These people must go to bed right after dinner, he thought. Nothing else to do but eat and sleep late. He turned back to the door and studied his reflection in the dark glass. It showed a tall, austere-looking man, fifty-five or so, with thinning white hair. The visored cap and blue uniform fit perfectly; he looked like an airline pilot or a naval officer.

Jimmy watched the cars again, humming softly under his breath. This was his first week as a doorman at the Hotel Pacific. They didn't pay much for the evening man, but it was better than the odd jobs he'd been doing, or running an elevator in a downtown hotel. He had seen the ad in the paper and phoned for an interview. The superintendent's name was Mr. King, and he needed someone immediately. His former doorman, a young fellow, had simply not come in, and Mr. King was determined to hire someone older and reliable to replace him. Fortunately, Jimmy was the right age and the uniform was the right size. The cars were still moving along Wilshire in the warm darkness. Jimmy speculated on them rather sadly, his head slightly bent, his hands clasped behind his back. He had lost out long ago, a victim of the vast indifference of circumstance. There wasn't much to look forward to, no wife for companionship and no money for simple indulgences. Just Social Security and a one-room walk-up in Santa Monica. Oh, well, he reflected, it could be worse. Better certainly, but it could be worse.

He walked across the lobby and looked through the glass wall into the courtyard. The apartments were built on three sides around a little green island of vegetation containing a swimming pool. The shrubbery was lit by pale violet lights and the pool was illuminated from below.

Jimmy stopped and squinted, polishing his spectacles. Someone was standing in the courtyard, bent over an oval fishpond. Who the devil would be feeding the goldfish at this hour, he wondered. Perhaps it was someone who had had too much to drink.

He opened the door quietly and walked around the shrubbery toward the pond. As he moved closer he could make out the figure of a woman. She was crouched down, leaning over the water. In her hand was a small goldfish bowl and she was dipping a mesh net in the pond.

"Excuse me, ma'am," Jimmy said.

The woman swung around, staring. "Who's there?" she said.

Jimmy went over to her. She was peering at him in the blue darkness, her eyes focusing behind thick glasses. She seemed to be in her mid-sixties, with a dry face and softly shining gray hair. "Who are you?" she asked.

"New doorman, ma'am. May I ask what you're doing?"

"Why, I'm taking my goldfish back," she said, indicating the bowl. Three fish swam in the water.

"Well, now, I'm sorry," said Jimmy gently, "but those fish are Mr. King's property. He wouldn't like any of the tenants taking them."

The old woman smiled. "I guess I should explain. These goldfish are mine. I usually put them in the pond with Mr. King's when I visit my sister in San Francisco."

Jimmy frowned at her. "I don't understand."

"It's a very simple arrangement. Mr. King feeds his fish every day. When I'm away I leave mine in the pool so they get fed with the others."

"Oh," said Jimmy, feeling a little foolish. "I didn't know that." He touched his cap. "Sorry to bother you, ma'am."

"Perfectly all right. I realize I must have looked as if I was stealing them. I just got back from San Francisco this evening and I wanted to take them in before it got too cold."

"I wouldn't think they're that sensitive, ma'am."

The old woman hugged the bowl protectively. "They're not really. But I like to pamper mine."

Jimmy leaned against the rim of the pond and took out his pipe. "I used to own a few myself," he said thoughtfully. "They died, though. I came home from work one day and they were floating on top of the water. Probably didn't get enough oxygen."

"That's terrible," she gasped. "You should have put a water plant in their bowl. That gives them all the oxygen they need." She looked at him suspiciously. "Did you feed them every day?"

"Every day, ma'am. I guess it was the lack of a water plant."

The old woman nodded solemnly. Then she picked up her net. "Well, it's time to feed them. Good night."

"Good night," said Jimmy. "Sorry I startled you before."

She smiled vaguely at him and went off along the patio, holding the bowl tightly against her breast.

Jimmy lit his pipe and watched her enter the building. Nice old lady, he thought. Probably lives alone with her goldfish. He grew pensive, remembering the elderly people he had seen with dogs or cats. People get old, they need company, he decided. Human or animals, it doesn't make any difference. As long as they have something to take care of.

A light blinked on in the top floor of the building. A moment later the old woman moved across the window, carrying her precious bowl. Jimmy sighed and sat down on the stone edge of the pond, pulling absently on his pipe. Maybe I ought to pick up a few goldfish again, he thought. They're nice to come home to in the evening, give a touch of color to the place.

When the light went out Jimmy returned to the lobby. He knocked his pipe against an ashtray and went back to the glass doors to watch the cars heading toward the ocean.

Jimmy saw the old woman occasionally during the following weeks. Sometimes, at night, she would sit near the pond, inspecting the goldfish and tilting her head to feel the ocean breezes. Jimmy would join her, smoking his pipe, and they would chat for a few minutes in the darkened courtyard. The old lady always left early to feed her fish.

Every once in a while there were long stretches when he wouldn't see her at all. When he asked about her, Mr. King told him she was visiting her sister in San Francisco, and during these absences he would check the pond to see if she had left her goldfish with the others. They were always there, larger than the rest, swimming together in an aristocratic group of their own.

One evening, Jimmy was in the lobby when she came through the doors from the street. She was wearing a shabby black coat and she looked tired and irritable.

"Anything wrong, ma'am?" Jimmy asked politely.

"Just a little angry with myself. I went all the way to North Hollywood to buy some food for my goldfish, but the store wasn't open. I forgot that it closes on Fridays at six."

"Do you have enough to last through the weekend?"

The woman nodded wearily. "Yes. I'm sure there's plenty."

"You must feed them the best," said Jimmy, trying to cheer her up. "They certainly look healthy enough."

She nodded again, and Jimmy noticed that she didn't seem to be listening very carefully. Her eyes were on the dark street beyond the glass doors. "Jimmy," she said suddenly, "I'll be going up to visit my sister again soon, but I'm worried."

"Worried, ma'am?"

"I've been reading the papers lately about all those robberies along Wilshire. A lot of valuable things were stolen, even from hotels."

"I don't think there's any danger of that happening here," he said reassuringly.

"I know. But I can't help feeling that someone might break in while I'm away."

Jimmy laughed. "What could they take, ma'am? A few goldfish? You can always buy more of those."

The woman shook her head. "I have some things worth taking. That's the trouble."

Jimmy studied her. "Really?"

"My late husband was comfortably off. He left me some lovely things. Jewelry, silver. I have an original Cézanne." Her eyes lowered. "Now you're the only one who knows that besides my sister."

"They're insured, aren't they?"

"No. I never seem to get around to it."

Jimmy removed his pipe and packed it very carefully. "You ought to insure them, ma'am. I mean, the chances are pretty slim that someone would rob you, but you never know."

"That means I have to get them appraised first, doesn't it?"

"I guess so."

The old woman frowned. "I don't like that. Some strange man looking through my things. Still, it's wiser to be protected…"

Jimmy lit the pipe and watched her over the bowl. She stood thinking for a moment, then she walked to the door leading to the patio. She was about to go in when she turned. "Jimmy?"

"Yes, ma'am?"

"Would you do me a favor and keep an eye out the next time I visit my sister? Just check my door at night to see if it's locked. I'd appreciate it very much."

"Don't you worry, ma'am. I'll be happy to take care of it."

"Thank you," she said. "Good night, Jimmy."

"Night."

She moved slowly through the courtyard and into the building. A minute later the light went on, a yellow square in the violet shadows.

Jimmy smoked his pipe and concentrated on the window. A thought was growing in the back of his mind that he didn't like. He tried to think of other things, but the thought kept gnawing at his consciousness. Jewelry and an expensive painting in the old lady's apartment. All of it accessible and unprotected.

He grunted, angry at himself, and glanced away. What am I? he thought. A sneak thief? He looked up again and saw the window was still lit, bright and inviting. Uninsured jewelry. A French painting worth thousands. His teeth tightened on his pipe stem. It was impossible. How could the old woman have such valuable possessions? But why not? Her husband had been wealthy; they had probably lived in one of those elegant homes in Beverly Hills. After his death the house had been too large, too full of memories. She had moved into a small apartment, taking her goldfish and her Cézanne.

The window went dark. The foliage rustled in the courtyard, throwing high shadows against the building. It would really be very simple, Jimmy thought, mulling over the idea. All I'd have to do is wait until she visits her sister again. I can tell when she goes because she'll leave her goldfish in the pond. Then I'd go up to her apartment without qualms and open it with my house key.

It was ridiculous. What would you do with a French painting? Who, who would be insane enough to buy it? But there were probably outlets for such things. And the jewelry wouldn't be hard to get rid of, even though he'd have to sell it at a loss.

Jimmy smiled. Well, nothing like a daydream to revive the spirit and ward off loneliness. Sure, he'd rob the old woman, run away with her silver and jewelry and priceless French masterpiece. Of course. He laughed out loud and walked to the glass doors that overlooked Wilshire Boulevard. Jimmy, he thought humorously, you're a wicked man to be thinking such things.

The cars were moving endlessly toward the sea. The limousines and the wire-wheeled sports models. Jimmy stared at them. How much jewelry would it take to buy a new convertible? He leaned against the glass, his head swimming with astronomical figures, and he gazed at the cars.

The following Monday Jimmy woke in the early afternoon and went out for something to eat. Instead of returning to his apartment for his usual nap, he boarded a bus and rode through Beverly Hills along Wilshire Boulevard. It was a gray, overcast day, windless and hot. The bus rumbled past the muted glass façade of the Hotel Pacific and he rose to get off at the next corner.

The courtyard was colorless in the mid-afternoon haze, its shrubbery drained and pallid looking. Jimmy skirted the swimming pool and went toward the pond. A maid, coming from one of the ground apartments, called to him. "Hi, Jimmy."

He waved but he didn't stop to talk. The water in the pond was very still, and little shadows moved quietly in the depths like secret minnows. The old lady's goldfish were near the bottom, swimming in a tight cluster. Jimmy looked up at her window and saw that the shades were drawn. She must have left this morning for Frisco, he thought. Probably won't be back till the end of the week. He trailed his fingers through the warm water, thinking. Then he climbed the stairs to her apartment and rang the bell. No one came. He knocked on the door loudly, but there was no answer from inside.

And then, quite suddenly, he realized with a start of surprise that he actually intended to rob the place. Well, why not? Hadn't it been on his mind all along? Opportunity was too close to ignore; for the first time in his life all his desires, the vague and wistful longings, could be satisfied. And the price lay a few feet away behind the door. A moment later he had a plan worked out, simple and absolutely safe. He smiled and headed for the stairs.

He took the bus to his own apartment and rested until five o'clock. Then he strolled to the corner drugstore and dialed a number on the payphone.

"Hello?" said a heavy voice.

"This is Jimmy, Mr. King."

"What is it, Jimmy?"

"I'm afraid I won't be able to come in tonight, sir. I've been having some terrible cramps."

"Damn it," Mr. King said. "This is awful short notice."

"I know, but they just started to bother me."

"Well, maybe you'll feel better tonight, Might just be an upset stomach."

Jimmy paused. "No, I...I don't think so. I haven't been up to snuff for a week now, Mr. King. I think I may need a good checkup at the hospital."

"How long's that gonna take?"

"I don't know, sir."

Mr. King sounded irritated. "Okay, Jimmy. I'll get somebody for tomorrow night. Trouble is, nobody will be on tonight."

"I'm sorry, Mr. King."

"That's okay. You take care of yourself."

Jimmy hung up. There was still a problem, a big one. He needed a car, that was a necessity. He couldn't get on a bus with a painting under his arm. He'd have to rent a car just for the evening.

In downtown Los Angeles he ate a small dinner and walked to the nearest office of a Rent-A-Car garage. He signed papers, paid a deposit, and drove off the lot in a convertible with wire-spoked wheels. It was an extravagant choice but it seemed an appropriate one given the circumstances. He joined the other cars on Wilshire and shot out to the green tip of the Pacific. It was warm twilight now, and the sky seemed to have opened wide over the beach. Riding with the top down in a rush of other sleek machines, he felt as if he was a member of a powerful new fraternity. He raced the car to eighty, then checked his excitement and braked to a legal sixty. This was not the night to be detained for speeding.

It was a few minutes after eleven when he parked near the Hotel Pacific. The lobby gleamed emptily, its doors closed for the night. He walked cautiously around to the back and entered the courtyard. There were no lights visible in any of the apartments. Moonlight made a round white coin of the little pond. Well, he thought, this is it. And if anyone catches me I'll just say I was checking for the old lady.

He entered the building and quietly climbed the tile stairs. He paused at the top and listened. Everything was perfectly silent, not even the late-night talk of a television set. He edged up to the door and leaned against it, waiting. He rang the bell, just in case, and the chimes echoed hollowly inside the apartment. He inserted his house key and turned the lock, waiting again to see if anyone had heard the sound. Then he touched the door and it swung open slowly.

At first glance he thought he had gone to the wrong apartment. There was no furniture in the living room, only large glass cases glimmering faintly in the moonlight. Puzzled, he closed the door behind him and looked around. Hundreds of tiny, flat eyes seemed to examine him from behind the glass walls. There were racked tiers of aquariums, rows of them, all containing tropical fish. He had never seen so many different species, so many bizarre colors rippling in the dull light. Most of them were small, with strong jaws and sharp teeth. They spun lazily through the water, bright spirals of bronze and blue.

But there's nothing else here, he thought. No painting, no silverware, just a bed and these hundreds of fish. Why had she told him about the Cézanne and the silver and jewelry? The palms of his hands suddenly felt very cold. What about the doorman before him, the young fellow. Hadn't he phoned in to Mr. King one afternoon and never returned?

Jimmy himself steadied himself with care against one of the glass cases. Everything had been planned for him. The conversations with the old lady, the fake trip to San Francisco, the lure of valuable things. He looked down at the fish swimming in the heated water. All of them were plump and well-fed. He remembered hearing somewhere about a fish called the Piranha, a creature so voracious, and with such sharp teeth...

Then he heard the door opening softly behind him.

EXIT LINE

Arthur St. Clair left his seat before the curtain calls and made his way through the empty lobby. The audience was still clapping furiously as he came out into the damp air and looked about for a taxi. A mounted policeman holding traffic grinned down from the height of his horse. "What's the verdict? Hit or miss?" And he grinned again.

St. Clair ignored him. A taxi moved smoothly along the curb and the driver held the door open. "Evening, sir," he said. St. Clair climbed inside, then leaned back and fitted a cigarette into a holder. He was a tall, coldly handsome man wearing a Chesterfield and Homburg. A columnist had once described him as a combination of "Brooks Atkinson and Brooks Brothers." He hadn't liked the label.

The taxi rumbled slowly through the growing theater traffic, but the cabby was silent during the ride. He had driven the critic to dozens of opening nights and knew the man's eccentricities well enough not to risk the loss of a tip. A few minutes later, when they reached the newspaper building on West 40th Street, St. Clair handed over a dollar and moved purposefully across the pavement, through the revolving doors.

The Features department was on the second floor, a long, untidy room with a few tired men sitting around on tables, drinking coffee. He nodded at them and went to his office near the elevator. It was an austere little room, its gray window decorated with a frieze of wet pigeons. The desk contained a typewriter, an ashtray, and the Strobl bust of Shaw. St. Clair removed his coat and hat and carefully limbered up his fingers. Then, without hesitation, he began to type the review he had composed in his head on the way from the theater:

"'*Enough Rope,*' *which opened last night at the Carlton, has serious merit, but it is disastrously flawed by the performance of Jack*

Russo, a wild and uninhibited young man who has learned everything about the theater except how to act. Mr. Russo is one of the so-called Method Men, a mumbling Tarzan who swings from one emotion to another as though from a vine. He strikes me as nothing more than a drugstore cowboy, a fifth-carbon Brando, who sees the theater not as a cathedral, but as a cave where he may grunt and beat his chest…"

St. Clair paused to light a cigarette and then looked up at the door. A young man stood in the entrance, watching him. He was short and squat, dressed in Levis and a faded windbreaker, his trousers tucked into muddy motorcycle boots. His flat, triangular face bloomed with a faint orange light that St. Clair recognized as makeup. The young man was obviously Jack Russo, and he must have run all the way from the theater to the newspaper office.

"Mr. St. Clair?" Yes, it was Russo, all right. The same dull, brutish tones that had dropped like rocks under the proscenium arch. "I came to read your review."

"I'm afraid that's impossible. You'll have to buy a paper like everyone else."

"But I came all the way over here – first thing, you know?"

"I appreciate that, Mr. Russo, but I can't make any exceptions. I'm sorry."

Russo slowly cracked each knuckle on his right hand. "You know what I think? I think you just gave me a hatchet job and you're too damned scared to let me see it."

St. Clair began to unroll the paper from his typewriter. "What I've written is none of your business until it hits the stands."

Russo suddenly snatched at the page. It tore, but he was left with the upper, crucial part. His small eyes swooped over the paper, blinked rapidly as he began to read.

"Give me that!" said St. Clair angrily. He stepped forward, but the actor put up a restraining arm. It seemed as solid and muscled as a truck driver's.

"Why, you louse," Russo said slowly. His eyes flicked at the paper again, re-reading. "Were you *there?* Did you see me tonight? Or were you home in bed?"

St. Clair was unruffled. "That's my review, take it or leave it. Now I'll give you two minutes to get out of this building before I call the police."

Russo stared at St. Clair blankly, as if he had spoken from a distant planet. Then he slowly crumpled the paper into a small, hard ball and savagely hurled it at the desk. It glanced off Shaw's mouth and went rolling away on the bare floor. He looked at St. Clair, his face stiff, then he turned abruptly and went out.

St. Clair cleared his throat and lit a cigarette. Without bothering to retrieve the crumpled paper, he sat down at the desk and began to retype the review from memory.

The following noon he took a cab to Sardi's and was shown to his favorite table. He started to run his eyes down the menu when he had the vague feeling that someone was watching him. He lowered the large card and looked out over the bright dining area, immediately recognizing Jack Russo and a heavy older man seated near the entrance. Russo was glaring across at him while his companion, leaning close, seemed to be arguing in a low voice. A few moments later, Russo rose, threw down his napkin, and stalked out.

St. Clair relaxed, lighting a cigarette. He ordered and looked out over the busy room, noting one or two Hollywood people and the usual gathering of tourists.

"Mr. St. Clair?"

Russo's companion was standing next to the table. Close up, he was a surprisingly ugly man, his face blunted and veined. Dandruff powdered the lapels of his cheap business suit. St. Clair frowned at him.

"Yes?"

"I'm Bert Lyons, sir. Jack Russo's agent and personal manager."

St. Clair grunted. "What can I do for you, Mr. Lyons?"

"I guess you haven't heard," he began awkwardly, "but Jack took your review pretty hard. I've never seen him like this before, it's like he's ready to blow up or something."

"That's too bad. If he can't face up to a bad notice he should be in some other business."

Lyons bent closer, and St. Clair had the distasteful feeling that the man was going to put a pleading hand on him. "Mr. St. Clair, I'm not sure that Jack's entirely in the wrong. I've seen some pretty tough reviews in my time, but that one was out of the ordinary. In a way, I don't blame him for blowing his stack. What have you got against him?"

The critic sighed. "Nothing personal. I just don't think your client can act. He's totally unbelievable. I hate to think of people spending good money to see a dramatics club amateur. Now if you don't mind, I'd like to finish my coffee."

Lyons stared hard at the carpet. "Mr. St. Clair, if I could get to the real reason I wanted to talk to you...I was wondering..."

"Wondering what?"

"If maybe you could, well, apologize to Jack. Just tell him you didn't think he was right for this particular role."

St. Clair looked up, astonished. "Are you serious?"

"I thought that might calm him down. Ever since last night he's been acting like a madman. He won't even listen to me anymore."

St. Clair stood up and flung a bill on the table. "Good afternoon, Mr. Lyons. I advise you not to try anything like this again."

Lyons' voice was barely audible. "I'm sorry."

The critic hunted angrily for his coat-check. "For future reference – I don't write retractions. You can tell your client that."

He left Lyons at the table and retrieved his coat and hat from the girl.

Outside, snow was lightly falling on the canopy. "Cab, Mr. St. Clair?" the doorman asked.

He nodded. Then, suddenly, there was a sharp crack behind him, as if something heavy had fallen on the icy pavement. Russo was standing near the door, wearing a torn sheepskin jacket, his head bare. He had just dropped a stack of morning papers on the sidewalk. He jerked an arm at the column and defiantly cocked his head in a way that St. Clair mentally labeled as *vintage Rod Steiger.*

"See these?" Russo shouted, his breath exploding in the numbing air. "See them?" Several passers-by stopped to stare. "Eight reviews. All of them good – all of them *great!* Except one! You know who wrote the bad one? Huh? Answer me!"

A taxi angled in next to the curb and St. Clair quickly moved inside. But before it could pull away, the actor had pressed his face against the window. "You wrote it!" the round mouth shouted. "What do you have against me?" The cold glass began to cloud, wiping Russo out, but the gray lips came through clearly. "*What?*"

A moment later the cab shot away and St. Clair looked back. Lyons had appeared from nowhere and was trying to pull Russo away from the traffic. The two men stumbled across the pavement with the drunken lurch of amateur ice-skaters and St. Clair settled back in his seat.

That evening St. Clair gave a small dinner party at his apartment. It was a witty, candle-lit affair, the guest of honor a leonine English actor who had been recently knighted. The festivities ended around eleven, and St. Clair went downstairs to put his last guest in a cab. On the way back, in the empty elevator, he had a vague feeling of uneasiness. The Russo incident was still in the back of his mind, and he recalled the actor's hot face against the window, the suck of his lips on the glass.

As the elevator doors opened he had another feeling, sharper this time, as he saw how he had left his apartment door wide open. He went in and locked the door, double-chaining it. The long rooms were dimly lit, moving with blue shadows from the falling snow outside. A few candles still burned on the dinner table among the discarded food and wine glasses.

St. Clair rubbed his eyes and he decided to go to bed. He walked slowly through the living room toward the back chamber and then noticed, from the corner of his eye, that someone was sitting in the deep leather chair in the corner. He whirled around, staring at the wide pool of shadow surrounding the chair. Two trouser legs jutted out on the carpet, their owner wearing boots that glimmered damply with snow.

"Russo? Is that you?" He came closer and recognized the actor, slumped down in the chair, wearing the sheepskin coat.

"How did you get in here?"

The actor thought about this for a few moments, then mumbled tonelessly, "The door was open."

"Well, get out."

The eyes blinked dully. "Aren't you going to offer me a drink?

Here I walked all the way from the Village and I'm wet and cold and tired and you won't even give me a drink. What kind of a host is that, Mr. St. Clair?"

The critic strode angrily to the door and jerked it open. "I want you to leave."

Russo slowly unfolded his bulk from the chair and got to his feet. Now St. Clair could see that there was a faint, far-off smile on his face. Wavering slightly, the actor made his way to the dinner table and picked up a decanter of brandy. "I haven't eaten since yesterday," he said. "No, that's wrong. Correction. I had a hot dog at Redick's." He sloshed some of the liquor into a soiled glass. "What did *you* have to eat, Mr. St. Clair?"

The critic didn't answer.

Russo poked around the table. "I asked you a question," he said pleasantly. "What did you have to eat?"

"I told you to get out."

The actor peered at one of the dinner plates, sniffing at it. "Hors d'oeuvres. Not bad. And what's that stuff on the little crackers? I'll bet that's caviar. Am I right, Mr. St. Clair? Isn't that caviar?"

The critic went to the telephone and picked up the receiver. But the line was dead; there was no sound of a dial tone. He looked down at the baseboard and saw that the wire had been brutally ripped from the wall. Russo closed the door and chained it. "I don't like telephones," he said. "They're an invasion of privacy. Don't you agree?"

St. Clair went toward the door. "I'm going to get the doorman," he said quietly.

Russo blocked his way. "But you can't leave now. I thought we were going to have a nice long talk."

St. Clair lunged at the door, tried to get it open. But Russo was there before him. The critic turned and quickly headed for the bedroom.

"Don't bother about that other phone in there," Russo called. "I took care of that one too."

St. Clair returned to the living room. Russo had pulled the chair in front of the door and was now comfortably seated, legs crossed, picking at a plate of hors d'oeuvres.

"What do you want from me?" St. Clair asked wearily.

"I want to talk, that's all. Let's have a good, old-fashioned bull session. I mean, it's not often a nobody actor like me gets to talk to one of New York's foremost theater critics."

"What do you want, Russo? A written retraction? An apology?"

"No." His face changed. "I don't want any of those things. I just want to fill you in on somebody's history. Mine."

St. Clair poured a glass of brandy from the decanter. The glass stopper tinkled faintly in the neck as he set it down.

"What's wrong?" Russo said. "You nervous or something?"

St. Clair took a deep swallow, felt the pleasant, radiating warmth. "I'm ready to hear your piece. Then I expect you to clear out."

Russo got up and came over to him. His voice was hard. "I'll clear out when I'm good and ready. Understand?"

St. Clair nodded. He could feel his face growing hot.

"I'll tell you something, friend. I might look young, but I've been around. I started acting when I was twelve years old, all over the country. I didn't have any parents at the time and the theater was my home. You know what I mean?"

St. Clair nodded again.

"Say yes or no, Mr. St. Clair."

"Yes."

"Okay. So now you know I didn't make it in this business overnight. I've been acting all my life. And it isn't easy. You know, I flunked out of the Pasadena Playhouse? *Nobody* flunks out of there. But they taught me something I'll never forget. Guess what it was."

"I – I don't know."

"They said don't believe what anyone tells you about how good you are. That meant teachers, friends, or even critics. Especially the critics. And you're not the first guy that knocked me, St. Clair."

His hand dipped into his coat pocket and brought out a small revolver. "You see this?"

St. Clair swallowed. The barrel pointed at his right eye.

"I've been saving it for one of you guys," Russo said quietly. "You know where I got it?"

"No."

"One of my best friends took his life with it. This is the same gun. He had a lot of personal problems, but the critics didn't help. I figure wherever he is tonight, he'll get a big kick when he sees what I'm going to do."

"You're – joking." The tendrils of brandy had turned cold in his stomach.

"Don't you wish I was? No, tonight's the night, St. Clair. You know why?"

The critic shook his head.

"Because you hate me. You probably wanted to be an actor yourself one day. But you didn't make it. You didn't have the talent or the guts. And that's why you try to destroy young guys like me. If you don't make it, nobody does. Well, I'm not going to stand around while you write my obituary. I know right now that every time I open in this town you're going to get me. That's the kiss of death for an actor. Pretty soon producers get the idea and I stop getting parts in their plays."

St. Clair looked down at the gun. It seemed as smooth and guileless as a child's toy. He tried to be impassive, but he could feel his face going white.

"So maybe tonight we were fooling around with a gun and you had an accident. I mean, you got a little drunk at your dinner party, and the next thing – wham! It happens all the time."

St. Clair examined the man's eyes. They were very flat and steady, each one burning with a small pinpoint of light.

"What's wrong, St. Clair? All that caviar upset your stomach?" The gun inched closer.

The critic moved back across the table, his arm reaching behind him, scattering glasses. The man intended to kill him. If there was only some weapon he could use… something to protect himself with.

"Why's your face so wet, St. Clair? I always thought critics made other people sweat."

His fingers, still reaching, touched the rough, diamond-cut edge of the liquor decanter.

"You're really scared, aren't you? Maybe I can put you out of your misery."

The critic swung the decanter, hitting Russo directly between the eyes. The actor blinked once, as a tiny red blister appeared on his forehead, then he fell solidly, bumping on the thick carpet.

St. Clair leaned over the table, almost physically sick. He stood there for a few minutes, still holding the glass decanter. Then he looked down at Russo. The actor lay at the foot of the table, his mouth open as if in heavy sleep. It suddenly occurred to St. Clair that the man had stopped breathing. He bent over him and opened the sheepskin coat, felt inside the shirt. No, it couldn't be. He hadn't hit him that hard. But the chest was still, not even a heartbeat.

St. Clair stood up, holding the little revolver in his hand, first confused then startled. What does one do when something like this happens? He supposed he should notify the police immediately. It meant going downstairs and using one of the payphones. He was still standing over Russo when the doorbell rang, a bright tinkle that came again and again in waves.

Dazed, almost sleepwalking, St. Clair went to the door and unlocked it. Outside was Bert Lyons, his face bursting with a grin. With him were two newspaper reporters and a photographer trying not to look guilty.

"Well?" Lyons cried. "Did he fool you? Wasn't he great? And you were the guy who said Jack Russo couldn't act!"

St. Clair stared at them, then involuntarily his finger pulled the trigger. The hammer clicked harmlessly on the empty chamber.

Still grinning, Lyons swept past him into the apartment. "Jack?" he called. "Where are you?"

THE MAN IN THE LOBBY

It had been a wasted morning for Wolfson. The captain had sent him over to the Golden Gate Hotel to check out a public nuisance complaint, but after a brief investigation he found that it was groundless – a few conventioneers had blundered into the wrong room after a night of carousing.

He left the elevator and glanced at the people coming in from Powell Street. It was not quite noon, but the hotel bar was already crowded with advertising men from the cluster of office buildings a few blocks away. All riding the expense account, he imagined. What would it take to pull them away from their martinis and black Russians? A stock market crash, probably. Either that or another earthquake.

Well, it was time to report back. As he started across the busy lobby, he brushed by a man at the check-in desk. The face hung for an instant in his mind, then he dismissed it. At the street door he hesitated and turned back. The man at the desk was in his early fifties, meek and rumpled, with the slightly dazed expression of someone who had spent his life in front of a blackboard or an adding machine. He wore a cheap summer suit and a frayed blue shirt.

Wolfson strolled back to the counter and tried to get a better look.

"Anything on the twelfth floor?" the man was saying.

"Twelve-Oh-Five is available," said the desk clerk. "Nice and spacious." He slipped a registration card into a leather folder and pushed it across the counter. "There's a lovely view of the pagodas on Grant Street."

The man mumbled something, then signed the card and started for the elevators. Wolfson, no more than a casual foot away, instantly made the connection. He took his wallet from his back pocket and crossed to the man, tapping him on the shoulder. "San Francisco Police," he said, showing his badge. "Sorry to bother you, sir, but would you mind telling me your name?"

The little man blinked at him from watery eyes. "Miller," he said in a fuzzy, classroom voice. "Charles Miller."

"Mind waiting here a moment, Mr. Miller?"

Wolfson went to the desk and opened his wallet again. "I'd like to see this gentleman's registration card, please."

The clerk produced the information. "Charles Miller, 10337 Lombard Street, San Francisco."

Wolfson copied down the address and returned the card. When he swung back to Miller, the little man was staring vaguely up at the hotel clock, idly jiggling the room key.

"You live here in San Francisco, don't you, Mr. Miller?"

"Yes." The voice seemed on the verge of disappearing.

"Then why are you checking into a hotel?"

Miller shrugged. "Business."

"What kind of business?"

Miller looked up again at the clock, as if he were a small boy waiting impatiently for a recess.

"What kind of business, Mr. Miller?"

"I have to meet a few people. Salesmen, mostly."

Wolfson glanced at the carpet. "And no luggage?"

"Just overnight."

Wolfson studied his face closely. Could he be mistaken? Was there a chance that this was a look-alike, a near-perfect double? There was a tiny white scar just below Miller's left eye that seemed to underscore the man's essential blankness. That scar and the rest of the description could be checked by Teletype this afternoon.

"I'm afraid I'm going to have to ask you for some identification."

After a slight pause the man patted most of his pockets and finally fished an old wallet from somewhere inside his jacket. He held it out.

"No, you go through it. Social Security card, driver's license. Anything."

The man thumbed through a small packet of cards and handed him a license. It was State of California issue and the name was Charles Miller.

As Wolfson studied it a group of bystanders had begun to gather, trying to edge closer.

"Sorry to trouble you like this, Mr. Miller, but I'd like you to come with me. It shouldn't take more than a half-hour or so."

The little man looked wistfully at the elevators. "But I thought I could…" His voice threatened to disappear again. "Is it important?" he asked.

"I've got a car outside. It'll be as quick as I can make it."

"Well…I suppose so." He looked down at the key in his white, plump hand. "What should I do?"

Wolfson began to feel sorry for him. "You've already registered. They'll hold the room for you." He guided the man to the door. "You'll be back in plenty of time to keep your appointments."

Outside in the bright, almost holiday air, Miller seemed dazed and lost. A cable car jangled, and he stiffened upright with the sound. Wolfson took his arm and led him up the hill, watching him carefully. The man was blinking hard in the glittering sunlight, but he looked more bewildered than trapped.

When they reached the automobile Wolfson held open the door, then got in and started the engine, throwing his companion a quick, assessing glance. The man was staring down at his hands, still toying with the key.

"Mr. Miller," Wolfson said, driving toward Market, "there's one thing that bothers me. You haven't once asked why I'm taking you in."

Miller shrugged listlessly. They were passing Union Square and a pigeon sprang gray and frightened across the windshield.

"Why aren't you interested?"

"I imagine I'll find out."

"I imagine you will." It would take only a short time to verify, but he was pretty sure Miller wouldn't be returning to his hotel.

He parked the car a block off Market and walked the little man up the steps of the station house. There was no one in the squad room, just a few stale newspapers and the smell of new paint. He left Miller alone in the interrogation room and went down the corridor to Sy Pagano's office.

Pagano was leaning on the windowsill, looking up at the sky. "I haven't seen a gull in three weeks," he said. "You think it's the fallout or something?"

Wolfson didn't bother closing the door. "Got something, Sy."

"Yeah?"

"Brought in a man by the name of Charles Miller. I think it's an alias."

Pagano was looking up at the sky again. "Who do you think it is?

"Frederick Lerner. The schoolteacher from Santa Barbara who killed those two women last week."

Pagano turned abruptly from the window. "Are you sure it's him?"

"The description fits. L.A. sent a wire-photo up yesterday. They mentioned he might have headed for San Francisco."

"Where'd you spot him?"

"The Golden Gate Hotel. He was checking in without luggage."

Pagano picked up the phone and punched a button. "I'll call L.A., get more information. Where've you got him?"

"Interrogation." Wolfson went out and walked back to the other office. Miller was sitting in a chair, looking at the wall. His eyes squinted slightly in the bright rush of light from the window. Wolfson drew the shade and sat down with him. He took his time lighting a cigarette. "Sorry. You want one?"

"I don't smoke."

"How long have you lived in San Francisco, Mr. Miller?"

The little man rubbed his eyes. "Only a few weeks."

"Where did you live before that?"

"New York. My company sent me out here."

Wolfson got up, went back to the window. There was no one in the street beneath the half-lowered shade. A church clock chimed the hour and he checked it with his watch. "What line of work are you in, Mr. Miller?"

"Heavy goods jobbing."

"Married?"

There was a pause while chimes succeeded each other like ripples in water. "Yes, I'm married."

"Happen to have a picture of your wife?"

"Is it important?"

Wolfson came back to him. The man's face was in half-shadow, but blinked up at the detective.

"It's important, Mr. Miller. Do you have one?"

The old wallet came out again. The man fumbled through the celluloid card folder, then held up a photograph. Wolfson took it over to the light. It was a crisp new picture of an attractive blonde, considerably younger than her husband. There was an interesting pout to her mouth. "Married long?" he asked.

"Few weeks."

The door opened and Pagano came in, carrying a file folder. "This is my partner, Mr. Miller, Lieutenant Pagano. You make that call, Sy?"

"Tried. The lines are tied up."

Wolfson took the photograph over to him. "This is Mr. Miller's wife."

Pagano studied it expressionlessly. He opened the file folder and removed two photos, tilting them so only his partner could see. "The victims," he said.

Wolfson touched the photos, moving them to catch the light. They both showed middle-aged women with vacant, trusting faces. Neither resembled the blonde.

"Your wife at home, Mr. Miller?" Pagano asked suddenly. It was his first acknowledgement of the man's presence.

"Yes."

Wolfson picked up the phone. "What's the number?"

Miller swung around quickly in the chair. "No – she's not at home. I made a mistake."

Wolfson met Pagano's eyes. "Oh? Where is she then?"

"She – left for Nevada this morning. Visiting some friends."

"I see. Has she got a phone number there?"

"No."

Pagano came around the side of the desk. "Stand up, Miller."

Miller got awkwardly to his feet.

"See that blackboard on the wall? Why don't you go over there and pick up that piece of chalk."

Miller did as he was told.

"Fine," said Pagano, glancing at Wolfson again. "Now write something on the blackboard."

The little man seemed ready to cry. "What should I write?"

"Anything. I don't care."

Miller was motionless for a moment, then his hand glided up and he wrote *Charles Miller* in a graceful, sweeping line. He started to turn around but Pagano called, "No, stay there. Write your name again."

While Miller wrote, Pagano took the wallet from his desk and dug out the driver's license. *Nice*, Wolfson thought. *Very nice.* Over Pagano's shoulder, he compared the signature on the card with the writing on the board. They matched.

"You're pretty good at that blackboard," Pagano observed. "Some of you guys would have that chalk squeaking like a mouse. But not you. You sure you're not a schoolteacher or something?"

"Well...I've had some experience with chalkboards," the little man said. He still faced away from them.

"Really?" Pagano said.

"Yes. Before my company sent me out here I was teaching some of the younger men, the sales trainees."

"But you never did any teaching at a school?"

"No."

Wolfson walked to the blackboard. "Here's another name. I want you to write 'Frederick Lerner.' Would you do that for me?"

The hand swung up without hesitation. It wrote the name in the same sure, graceful way.

"Uh-huh," Wolfson said. He went back to Pagano and gestured at the folder. Pagano opened it, and Wolfson removed another photo. He set it face up on the desk under the unlit lamp. "You can come back now, Mr. Miller. Have a seat."

The little man returned to the desk, blinking in confusion at them. He sat down wearily.

Wolfson pointed at the lamp. Mind turning on the light? I want to show you something."

Miller snapped the switch and then started, his hands gripping the arms of his chair. He was staring down at the photograph, a slow flush staining his face. "Where did you get that?" he said.

"From our files," said Wolfson. He and Pagano edged closer to the desk. "It's a picture of a man named Frederick Lerner. He killed two women in Santa Barbara last week."

"But – but that's a picture of me," Miller protested. He picked it up and stared. "That's *me*."

Pagano took the photo out of his hands. "The Los Angeles police got it from the yearbook of that private school where you used to teach."

Miller shook his head. "That's impossible. I was never in Santa Barbara in my life. Anybody can tell you that, anybody!"

"Can they?" Pagano said. "How about your new wife? Can she tell us that?"

Miller turned pale, almost the color of the photograph. He lowered his eyes and brought a cupped hand to his forehead. "There's been a mistake," he mumbled. "You've got me mixed up with someone else."

Pagano dropped down in the chair beside him. "Where'd you get that wallet, Lerner? Who is Charles Miller?"

"*I'm* Charles Miller!" The little man seemed close to tears. "You can ask my friends, my business associates. They can tell you."

Pagano leaned closer. "I think you're a liar. You killed those two women, and you came up here to hide. Look at me!"

"It's all a mistake! Can't you see that?"

Pagano's voice grew louder, more insistent. "I think you should make a statement. I think you should tell us about those two women."

"I don't know what you're talking about!"

Wolfson interceded. "Take it easy, Sy. We still don't have a positive identification."

"This guy is Frederick Lerner. The photo matches, he lied about having a wife, and he used the blackboard like a pro. I say book him."

Wolfson thought it over. For a moment he wished he had never recognized the man, had walked right by him.

"What do we do?" Pagano pressed. "Lock him up or let him go? Come on, buddy, make up your mind."

Wolfson looked down at the little man. He was holding the photo of Lerner again, studying it with dull incomprehension.

"Okay, we book him. I'm still not as sure as you are, but we can't take a chance."

"Take my word," Pagano said. "Everything checks."

"Let's go, Mr. Miller." Wolfson touched him gently on the shoulder. "Next stop is Fingerprints."

Miller nodded. He stood up and groped his way toward the door.

Pagano leaned against the windowsill, slapping the file angrily against his hip. "When you're finished," he said, "bring him back. I'm going to try L.A. again."

He was beginning to dial the phone when Wolfson closed the door.

At the fingerprint office Miller was disinterested as they rolled his fingers on the inked glass. Wolfson sat in a corner, smoking a cigarette and thinking. Something was wrong; Charles Miller – or whatever his name was – was too mild, too apathetic for a murderer.

A minute later there was a soft knocking at the door and Pagano looked in. "Wolfson? Could I see you?"

Wolfson followed him out, stamping his cigarette into the scarred floor. "You reach L.A.?"

"Yeah." Pagano didn't look at him directly. "They picked up Frederick Lerner last night."

"What?"

"Caught him hiding out in a friend's place near the U.C.L.A. campus. It's him, no chance of error."

Wolfson tried not to show his relief. "How do you like that?" he said. "The guy looks just like him. They could be twins."

Pagano sighed and held up his hands. "We goofed. We've done it before, we'll do it again. Look, you want to explain things to our friend in there? I'm not good on apologies. Tell him we're sorry, we made a mistake, the works." He grinned sourly. "You were always the diplomat. And give him a lift back to the hotel. He look like he's gonna collapse any minute."

It was a silent drive to the Golden Gate. Miller sat brooding in the front seat, completely withdrawn. He had taken Wolfson's apology blankly, once or twice looking at the smudge marks on his fingers.

"Tell you what," Wolfson said, trying to brighten the atmosphere. "We'll have a drink at the hotel. On me."

Miller shook his head. "No, thanks. You don't have to do that."

"All right, but don't you worry about anything. Nobody will ever know it happened. We didn't put you on the blotter so there's no record."

In the lobby of the Golden Gate Wolfson managed an awkward goodbye and sent the little man toward the bank of elevators. When the door slid closed he breathed a sigh of relief. The next time he would think twice before taking someone in for questioning.

He was about to leave when he heard his name being paged. There was a telephone call for him at the main desk.

Pagano was on the line. "Thought I could catch you there. On a hunch, I called Miller's place on Lombard. His wife answered."

Wolfson frowned. "I thought he said she was in Nevada."

"He lied. She's going to Nevada, all right, but not to visit friends. Reno, Nevada."

"She's divorcing him?"

"That's right. You should have heard her on the phone. Sounds like a real swinger. She said it broke him pretty bad but she doesn't care. Guess it was one of those May and December things."

"The poor guy," Wolfson said. "And we didn't make matters any easier for him."

"Yeah. Well, I thought you'd be interested. That'll be the last you ever hear of Mr. Charles Miller."

"Okay, Sy. Thanks."

He hung up and walked across the lobby to the doors on Powell Street. Well, it all figured. That's why Miller had seemed so indifferent and apathetic, even before he was asked to go downtown.

Outside, all along the curb, a crowd was beginning to gather. Cars had stopped and people were running up from the shops on Geary. Curious, Wolfson pushed through the door and looked up the steep stone slope of the hotel building. Miller stood on a ledge high up near the top, looking down at the crowd.

Now he knew why the little man had wanted a room on the twelfth floor.

EDITOR'S NOTE

The majority of these stories were credited on first publication to "William Link and Richard Levinson." (As was, for instance, their stage play *Prescription: Murder*.) Though the team is better known as Levinson and Link, the original attribution has been followed in this collection.

Bibliography
(in chronological order)

"Whistle While You Work" – *Ellery Queen's Mystery Magazine*, November 1954

"Child's Play" – *Alfred Hitchcock's Mystery Magazine*, January 1959

"Shooting Script" – *Alfred Hitchcock's Mystery Magazine*, April 1959

"Suddenly, There Was Mrs. Kemp" – *Alfred Hitchcock's Mystery Magazine*, April 1959 (by "Ted Leighton")

"Operation Staying-Alive" – *Alfred Hitchcock's Mystery Magazine*, July 1959

"Robbery, Robbery, Robbery" – *Alfred Hitchcock's Mystery Magazine*, August 1959

"The Hundred-Dollar Bird's Nest" – *Alfred Hitchcock's Mystery Magazine*, August 1959 (by "Ted Leighton")

"One for the Road" – *Escapade*, August 1959 (This is our chapbook for the limited edition)

"One Bad Winter Day" – *Alfred Hitchcock's Mystery Magazine*, September 1959

"Memory Game" – *Alfred Hitchcock's Mystery Magazine*, September 1959 (by "Ted Leighton")

"The Joan Club" – *Playboy*, November 1959.

"Dear Corpus Delicti" – *Alfred Hitchcock's Mystery Magazine*, March 1960

"Who is Jessica?" – *Alfred Hitchcock's Mystery Magazine*, August 1960

"No Name, Address, Identity" – *Alfred Hitchcock's Mystery Magazine*, July 1961

"The End Of An Era" – *Alfred Hitchcock's Mystery Magazine*, January 1962

"Top-Flight Aquarium" – *Alfred Hitchcock's Mystery Magazine*, April 1962

"Exit Line" – *Alfred Hitchcock's Mystery Magazine*, June 1962

"The Man In The Lobby" – *Alfred Hitchcock's Mystery Magazine*, June 1966

ACKNOWLEDGEMENTS

This collection would not have happened without the generous cooperation of William Link, his wife, Margery Nelson, his niece, Amy Salko Robertson, and Chris Levinson, Richard Levinson's daughter.

Jackie Sherbow and Deanna McLafferty of Dell Magazines kindly provided copies of the Link and Levinson stories which first appeared in *Ellery Queen's Mystery Magazine* and *Alfred Hitchcock's Mystery Magazine*.

Tom Straw stole time from his busy schedule to write a sterling foreword.

Honor Molloy cast her sympathetic editorial eye on the volume's contents.

Jeffrey Marks and Douglas G. Greene graciously welcomed the collection into the Crippen & Landru fold.

I am indebted to them all, and I offer them my deepest thanks.

SHOOTING SCRIPT AND OTHER MYSTERIES

Shooting Script and Other Mysteries by William Link and Richard Levinson is printed on 60 pound paper, and is designed by Jeffrey Marks using InDesign. The type is Jenson, an old-style serif typeface designed by Robert Slimbach. The printing and binding is by Southern Ohio Printing and Cincinnati Bindery for the hardcover and the trade paperback version. The book was published in October 2021 by Crippen & Landru Publishers, Inc., Cincinnati, OH.

Crippen & Landru, Publishers
P. O. Box 532057
Cincinnati, OH 45253
Web: www.Crippenlandru.Com
E-mail: info@crippenlandru.Com

Since 1994, Crippen & Landru has published more than
100 first editions of short-story collections by important
detective and mystery writers.

*This is the best edited, most attractively packaged line of
mystery books introduced in this decade. The books are
equally valuable to collectors and readers.* [Mystery
Scene Magazine]

*The specialty publisher with the most star-studded list is
Crippen & Landru, which has produced short story collections by some of the biggest names in contemporary crime
fiction.* [Ellery Queen's Mystery Magazine]

God bless Crippen & Landru. [The Strand Magazine]

*A monument in the making is appearing year by year from
Crippen & Landru, a small press devoted exclusively to
publishing the criminous short story.* [Alfred Hitchcock's
Mystery Magazine]

]

Recent Publications

Challenge the Impossible: The Impossible Files of Dr. Sam Hawthorne by Edward D. Hoch. Full cloth in dust jacket, signed and numbered by the publisher, $45.00. Trade softcover, $19.00.

Shooting Hollywood: The Diana Poole Stories by Melodie Johnson Howe.
Melodie Johnson Howe was "one of the last of the starlets," making movies with Clint Eastwood, Alan Alda, James Caan, James Farentino and others. Hollywood is brutal, and it is a place, as Marilyn Monroe said, "where they'll pay you a thousand dollars for a kiss, and fifty cents for your soul ..." Diana Poole finds crime in that world of glitz, glamour, and greed. Full cloth in dust jacket, signed and numbered by the author, $43.00. Trade softcover, $17.00.

Nothing Is Impossible: Further Problems Of Dr. Sam Hawthorne by Edward D. Hoch.
Dr. Sam Hawthorne, a New England country doctor in the first half of the twentieth century, was constantly faced by murders in locked rooms and impossible disappearances. *Nothing Is Impossible* contains fifteen of Dr. Sam's most extraordinary cases. Full cloth in dust jacket, signed and numbered by the publisher, $45.00. Trade softcover, $19.00.

Night Call And Other Stories Of Suspense by Charlotte Armstrong, edited By Rick Cypert And Kirby Mccauley. Lost Classics Series.
Charlotte Armstrong introduced suspense into the commonplace, the everyday, by writing short stories and novels in which one simple action sets a series of events spiraling into motion, pulling readers along, breathless with

anxiety. Full cloth in dust jacket, $30.00. Trade softcover, $20.00.

Chain Of Witnesses; The Cases Of Miss Phipps by Phyllis Bentley, edited By Marvin Lachman. Lost Classics Series. A critic writes, "stylistically, [Bentley's] stories ... share a quiet humor and misleading simplicity of statement with the works of Christie .... Her work [is] informed and consistent with the classic traditions of the mystery." Full cloth in dust jacket, $29.00. Trade softcover, $19.00.

Swords, Sandals And Sirens by Marilyn Todd.
Murder, conmen, elephants. Who knew ancient times could be such fun? Many of the stories feature Claudia Seferius, the super-bitch heroine of Marilyn Todd's critically acclaimed mystery series set in ancient rome. Others feature Cleopatra, the olympian gods, and high priestess Ilion blackmailed to work with Sparta's feared secret police. Full cloth in dust jacket, signed and numbered by the author, $45.00. Trade softcover, $19.00.

The Puzzles Of Peter Duluth by Patrick Quentin. Lost Classics Series.
Anthony Boucher wrote: "Quentin is particularly noted for the enviable polish and grace which make him one of the leading American fabricants of the murderous comedy of manners; but this surface smoothness conceals intricate and meticulous plot construction as faultless as that of Agatha Christie." Full cloth in dust jacket, $29.00. Trade softcover, $19.00.

The Purple Flame And Other Detective Stories by Frederick Irving Anderson, edited By Benjamin F. Fisher.
Previously uncollected stories by one of the premier mystery writers of the 1920's and the 1930's. Full cloth in dust

jacket, $29.00. Trade softcover, $19.00.

All But Impossible: The Impossible Files of Dr. Sam Hawthorne by Edward D. Hoch. Full cloth in dust jacket, signed and numbered by the publisher, $45.00. Trade softcover, $19.00.

Sequel to Murder by Anthony Gilbert, edited by John Cooper. Full cloth in dust jacket, $29.00. Trade softcover, $19.00.

The Island of Coffins by John Dickson Carr, edited by Douglas Greene and Tony Medawar. Trade softcover, $22.00

Never Trust a Partner by Robert Edward Eckels, edited and introduced by Brian Skupin, Full Cloth in dust jacket, signed and numbered by the author, $47.00. Trade softcover, $22.00

Hildegarde Withers: Final Riddles? by Stuart Palmer, introduced by Steven Saylor. Full Cloth in dust jacket, $32.00. Trade softcover, $22.00

Subscriptions

Subscribers agree to purchase each forthcoming publication, either the Regular Series or the Lost Classics or (preferably) both. Collectors can thereby guarantee receiving limited editions, and readers won't miss any favorite stories.

Subscribers receive a discount of 20% off the list price (and the same discount on our backlist) and a specially commissioned short story by a major writer in a deluxe edition as a gift at the end of the year.

The point for us is that, since customers don't pick and choose which books they want, we have a guaranteed sale even before the book is published, and that allows us to be more imaginative in choosing short story collections to issue.

That's worth the 20% discount for us. Sign up now and start saving. Email us at orders@crippenlandru.com or visit our website at www.crippenlandru.com on our subscription page.